DARK SECRETS

A novel by
Mabel Maglone Leo

Editor: K.M. Griffin
Author photo by
Ty Bass,
Wentworth Photograph

Cover photo courtesy of
Sailor Springs Historical Foundation
Cover design by Susie DePinto-Fraser,
Graph!c Statements, Inc.
ISBN 0-9650787-9-5

MIBS Publishing
P.O. Box 17413
Phoenix, AZ 85011-0413

Dear Readers,

Once again I thank all those who helped make this story live, particularly the Sailor Springs Historical Foundation, Sheriff Lee Ryker, and Coroner Gary Bright. And special thanks to the Daily Clay County Advocate-Press, and WNOI FM Radio for their kind book reviews.

Sincerely,

Mabel Maglone Leo

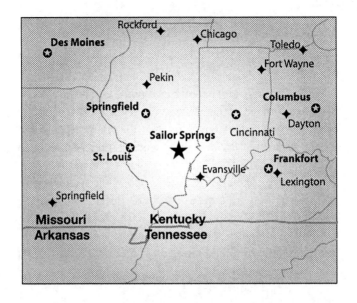

EPIGRAPH

"Soft Pond is a body of water on marshy land southeast of Sailor Springs and as long as anyone can remember, it has been a place of weird renown. Certain places at the bottom of the pond are soft, thus the name Soft Pond. Cattle and other stock while wading there have been known to sink and disappear never to be seen again, giving cause for belief that quicksand lies in the pond's bed, but then it could be that deep springs are responsible. It is truly said that the little meteoric lights, the will-o-the-wisps or jack-o-lanterns, were often seen at night as they bobbed along over the lowland."

Beryl Rinehart
Sailor Springs Story 1956

CHAPTER ONE

"You mean Charlie's body wasn't in the pond?" Sheriff John Brawley frowned, eyes scanning the mortuary office. "Practically the whole town saw him go under."

Police Chief MacLoone who most folks simply called 'Mac' stood beside the Sheriff." "No way he could have escaped that mud."

"Just what I said." Coroner Bill Hawkins explained. "Both divers did a thorough search of Soft Pond. Charlie wasn't there. Instead - - ."

The Chief cut in. "Instead what?"

"Human remains. I'm no forensic specialist but as near as I can tell whoever it is has been down there for - - " Bill scratched his ear, wanting to give the best quess he could, "maybe fifty years."

"Who?" Both lawmen demanded.

"Don't know yet. These things take time, guys."

Bill took up a computer printout from his cluttered desk. "The first three bodies were Charlie's victims, the waitress from the Blue Bird Café in Salem, Matt Kellum and Nancy Ann from Sailor Springs. The last one was not Charlie Doyle, or Chuck Bolden, whichever you want to call him."

Anticipating their next question, he explained, "DNA might be possible using a bit of the marrow taken from the victim's femur. That would take a couple of weeks. Or, assuming the victim was local, and if there is enough teeth or pieces of teeth that can be matched to dental records, we might make a identification."

He let that sink in before adding, "Apparently the body was placed in a plastic bag before being thrown into the water. The bag had torn open, some body parts are missing, but - I've saved the best part for last - the skull is intact, at least enough for reconstruction."

"Bingo." John grinned, taking a newspaper Bill handed over, pointing to a front page article. "This gal lives in Carbondale, semi-retired, works if the case catches her interest."

His friends scanned the photo of a pleasant-looking woman in her early sixties, short white hair, friendly eyes.

"She's worked with the Chicago Police. You're the one to talk to her, John. See if she'll take this on, get us a face, we're half way home. And get whatever else you've got off to the lab in Carbondale ASAP. See what they come up with. " The Sheriff added, "Mark it urgent, sign my name. They owe me some favors down there."

"But", Mac asked. "What about Charlie?"

"Finding his body is now your job."

"Better let the State boys know, in case they run across a victim in dry dock." John grinned. "They'll give us a bad time over losing a body but can't be helped."

Mac clamped onto his friend's shoulder. "Unless he's stuffed in a freezer, got to be damn smelly when we do find him. Maybe it'd be best to let them find it."

"We got a good relationship going. Don't want to screw it up over a dead body."

"If we find it first, nothing wrong with keeping it to ourselves, dropping a few hints their way.

"They'll love making us look bad. Better than dealing with that mess."

"Mac, you are downright nasty sometimes." John winked at Mac and Bill. "Let's keep this under wraps as long as we can."

Sheriff John Brawley, Police Chief Sean MacLoone, and Clay County Coroner Bill Hawkins had been friends since babyhood. They'd seen bodies pulled from lakes, ponds, rivers, bloated bodies, partially eaten by turtles and fish, body parts missing, faces twisted in frozen suffering, frothing from the mouth, bodies parched white. This time it was not strangers but their friends, neighbors waiting in steel mortuary coolers, all homicides. There would forensic specialists coming from Springfield, numerous reports to write. And Charlie to be found.

CHAPTER TWO

Norma woke from dreams of Jack smiling as she walked towards him on their wedding day. She savored the memory, tainted by visions of a casket, her husband's smile that never failed to melt her heart gone - forever. And Frank coming to her, the touch of his hands drawing her close, lips briefly, gently touching hers.

She gazed leisurely around the room, antique dresser, floor lamp next to an overstuffed chair a small lamp, notepad and pen, braided throw rugs on the wooden floor. Home, sweet home.

Throwing back the heavy quilt, she crawled over white cotton sheets to the foot of the bed, stretched until fingertips reached the white lace curtains, pushing them aside, expecting to see frost turning the fields glistening white, trees of gold and red leaves, autumn in southern Illinois at its best. Instead grey fog covered the world.

Wrapping herself in the thick chenille robe, she hoped Nell was in the kitchen, not in the barn tending to her sheep. The answer came with fresh coffee's aroma teasing at her nose. With a few flicks of the brush to her newly-cropped hair, Norma wondered if Frank would like it. Men preferred long hair but Frank wasn't like other men. She frowned at her reflection, voices shouting in her head.

Just a cotton-pickin' minute. You let some jerk in high school knock you up and you gave the baby up for adoption, your mother died after a battle with cancer and your father drank until he got up the nerve to put a gun to his head, splattering his useless brains all over the place, your first husband liked kinky sex with boys and girls, your second husband, the best decision of your whole life died, you went on to become a damn good writer, then you fell into bed with a guy you haven't thought of for 30 some years and he tried to kill you and now you're worried about whether or not this Frank DeCani guy will like your hair short? You are kidding, aren't you?

She leaned forward, sneering into the mirror. *Shut up. All of you. Just shut up!*

+ + + + +

Nell, in her usual garb of faded bib overalls and plaid flannel shirt, watched the slow dripping of brewing coffee. Floorboards creaked above the kitchen. It felt good to have someone in the house, especially a childhood friend. She was glad she'd snuck out of the house earlier without waking Norma.

With the families and friends of Charlie's victims, Nell had watched the bodies brought out of the pond, thankful the divers had wrapped them in black plastic bags before bringing them to the surface.

When the Coroner released the bodies there would be funerals to attend and life could begin again for the survivors.

Norma had suffered enough. She didn't need to be at Soft Pond, once only a place where wandering cows disappeared into the thick mud. Now a place of death, human deaths caused by her former lover.

She peered out the window over the sink, shivering at the cold grey mist stubbornly clinging to the earth.

Now Norma had a man who truly loved her. *Perhaps soon I, too, will have a new love .Bard. Bard Bolden. Who'd athunk it? A big city boy falling for a country hick?*

They'd talked about being business partners, turning her house into a bed-and-breakfast and the next thing she knew he asked for permission to court her. Wonder of wonders.

"Coffee smells delicious." Norma wrapped her chenille-covered arms around Nell.

"How are you?"

"As grey as the weather." Norma grabbed a cup, finger trailing words on it's surface, 'Tis herself' "An Irish cup. I love it."

"Picked it up at a yard sale." Nell watched as Norma filled the cup. "When is Frank coming back?"

"Soon, I hope."

"He loves you." Nell sipped at her coffee, waiting for her friend's answer. "You love him?"

Though Norma didn't use sugar or cream, she stirred the coffee, concentrating on its rich, brown swirls.

Nell tried again. "Having doubts?"

"Some."

"Scared?"

"Some."

Nell pushed a plate of brownies across the table. "Chocolate is good for the soul. Sit."

"Dessert for breakfast. I like that."

Norma secretly allowed herself all the chocolate she wanted when working on a novel. "Love your kitchen. It's so warm, comfy."

"So country?" Nell brought the dessert plates, served them each a large piece of the decadent chocolate.

"So real. Life can be so phony."

"Frank does love you. It showed every time he looked at you."

"Maybe he's just a good actor. Men are good at acting to get what they want."

"It's understandable you'd feel that way. But Bard has known Frank for years. He's genuine."

"But am I? I took to Charlie's charade like those lonely, love-starved pitiful widows I swore I'd never be."

Norma leaned back in the chair. "And what did I do? Jumped into bed with a married man, a man I didn't really know. What's that say about me?"

"Have you asked yourself what it says about Frank? He knows and still loves you, wants to marry you."

Nell's stoic face made Norma laugh. "You, my friend, should have been a therapist."

"No sense wasting words when the truth is so easy." She repeated, "You love him?"

"That's the kicker. I'm not sure. Guess it's not him I don't trust. It's me." Normal glanced at the clock above the sink. "You went without me."

Nell busied herself cutting more brownies, refilling her cup. "You didn't need to be there."

"I owe them."

"You don't owe anybody. You're one of us, of them."

"Those women at the pond, they saved my life." Norma's head dropped. "I still can't believe it."

"Thunder had a lot to do with it, too." Nell reminded her. "Jerked the leash right out of my hand. When he leaped at Charlie I was afraid he'd

end up in the pond, too, but thank God he stopped in time."

Norma looked up. "Did I ever thank him?"

"Profusely." Nell laughed. " You wanted to feed him steak for the rest of his life."

That brought a smile to Norma's face. "I remember so little of - - - ."

"No wonder, my dear. Now, what is on your slate for today?"

A jumble of thoughts attacked Norma's mind. How long had it been since nothing, absolutely, unbelievably nothing was expected of her. No editor tearing her precious words apart, no publisher screaming "Deadline! Deadline!" No publicist demanding her appearance at another worth-while fundraiser.

She threw her hands in the air. "Nothing! I have nothing to do today!"

"You are such a stitch." Nell laughed again. She didn't laugh much anymore. It felt good. "Get your little self upstairs, take a hot shower and - and - go for a walk. Take a nap. Just get out of my kitchen. I've got things to do even if you don't."

"Yes, Mama." Norma planted a quick kiss on her friend's cheek. "I'm gone."

Nell busied herself in the kitchen where something always needed washing or drying or wiped off or put away, waiting to be close in case Norma wanted anything. She'd gone directly upstairs. Perhaps she'd gone back to bed.

+ + + + +

Instead of slipping under the comfy quilt Norma sat on the edge of the bed wondering what to do with all this free time fate handed her. She couldn't remember the last time she didn't have a definite plan in mind for the day. No story pushing her towards the computer, no research to be done, no shopping, cleaning, paying bills, book signings, or meetings. Nothing. A flicker of movement caught her eye. Her gaze locked on Grandma's manuscript. *Trying to tell me something, Grandma?*

A hot shower, a quick cold-water rinse was just the ticket to get her ready for the world.

Maybe later, before going to bed, she'd soak in a hot tub with a glass of wine. How long had it been since she did that? Too long.

Showered and dressed, foregoing makeup, she did a check-up in the floor-length mirror. Denim pants, jacket, embroidered hummingbirds running across the back, tailored white shirt underneath, she told the reflection, "A country girl at heart."

Ignoring the cell phone on the dresser, she tucked the sheaf of papers under an arm and took to the stairs.

Nell heard her coming, waited in the kitchen. "How about another cup of coffee?" she called out, sensing Norma had reached the last step.

"No thanks. Think I'll read for a while, maybe take the dogs for a walk. Okay?"

"Sure. I'll be in the barn."

"Okay." Norma shouted back, grateful for the privacy.

Stepping out onto the front porch Nell's dogs came bounding at her. Black and tan, the huge dogs had wandered onto the property one stormy night. Nell appropriately named them Thunder and Lightening.

At sight of her, the dogs leaped, paws reaching her shoulders. "Okay, boys. If you're good, we'll go for a walk later. Right now I have reading to do. Deal?"

As though understanding, they leaped over the porch steps chasing a barn cat who prudently dashed up a tree, leaving the dogs running circles below.

She retreated from the chilly air to the glass-enclosed porch, cuddling into a corner of the paisley couch with the afghan in similar colors draped over its back.   Nearby sat a wooden icebox.   She smiled at memories it brought back, summer at Grandma's, the iceman coming twice a week.

She and her baby sister always argued who would place the card of colors in the front window; red for 100 pounds of ice, green for 50, blue for 25, yellow for 10, Lori Anne pouting that it was her turn and even though Norma was certain it wasn't she usually gave in.

A kind of peace descended as she began reading the familiar handwriting. She snuggled deep into the afghan's warmth.

Two hours later she put "Stars in Her Crown" aside. Grandma wrote of a love between two people whose heavy family responsibilities kept them from marrying, saving a few hours each week for one another at a secret place on the Spring Grounds.

Norma felt Grandma's grief when her lover died, shared her sorrow. The sadness overwhelmed her.   She shook herself free from its spell, went outside to fresh air, a new day.

Greeted again by Thunder and Lightening, she strolled slowly down the driveway lined with brown and yellow mums, the dogs racing back and forth, running through the fields, noses to the ground, hunting for what, she wondered.

A covey of quail rising out of brush along the road answered her. The clear air seemed to sparkle in the sunlight. Shivering, she picked up the pace, swinging her arms in cadence.

What could she say to Frank when he did come? The day he left for Phoenix he asked her to wait for him.

Did he still feel the same? How did she feel?

Despite misgivings about getting involved with him or any man, her heart quickened at the thought of seeing his smile that lit up a room and those dancing eyes that made everyone near him return the smile.

There had been no smile, no dancing eyes when she'd told him how Charlie beat her and again when Charlie masturbated on the skylight above the solarium. Frank's face turned hard, jaw clenched, his brown eyes suddenly coal black.

Forget about them. Forget about men, she told herself. *Get back to Grandma's story. Concentrate on that.*

She followed the dogs until reaching a fork in the road. Her head turned as she looked down the road running from the field behind Nell's house to the deep woods in the distance and Soft Pond. Charlie.

Charlie dragging her from the field to his truck, tying her, taking her to the cemetery and the crypt where he ravished her viciously, forced her to the pond. No one knew she was there. Her plan to trap him had failed. Frank, Bard, everyone looking in the wrong places, she would die.

Then women came from the thick forest in house dresses, bathrobes, faded Levis. They surrounded the pond brandishing sledgehammers, scythes, crowbars, rifles, hunting knives stained with generations of animal blood.

Nell had let Thunder track Charlie and Norma from the cemetery to the pond. The dog's instincts raged at the sight of Charlie holding Norma captive, knife at her throat. He lunged forward, sliding to a sudden stop at the pond's edge. Startled, Charlie jumped back,, falling into the murky water.

Norma shivered at the terrible thoughts of that day. "Let's go home, boys," she told Thunder and Lightening. The dogs obediently turned and headed back, driving pheasants skyward.

CHAPTER THREE

One of the few not at Soft Pond that day was Otho Helmutt. He knew about Charlie's murderous spree but had more important things to do like picking up a few bucks doing odd jobs around town. After graduating from high school he'd gotten in trouble one too many times and his dad threw him out of house.

Luckily Aunt Betty took him in. She treated him good but her waitress job at the Early Bird Café didn't pay much. If he wanted money, he earned it.

The young man dreamed of being a lawman, like Sheriff John Brawley. Nobody messed with the Sheriff. Encouraged by his aunt and with his idol's permission, Otho visited the Sheriff's office often, doing whatever odd jobs he could, hoping to learn more about law enforcement through an informal apprenticeship until he had enough money for college.

He was sitting at the Sheriff's secretary's desk while she ran personal errands when the Coroner and the Chief of Police came in.

After brief hellos and the two men in the Sheriff's office behind closed doors, Otho hurried to the store-room. With an ear to the wall, he could hear what went on in the Sheriff's office.

He heard about Charlie's body missing from the pond, how they planned to keep it secret. Caught up in the excitement of knowing what he wasn't supposed to, Otho didn't get back to the secretary's desk before Sheriff Brawley's visitors came out of his office.

Mac took one look at the surprised look on Otho's face and nabbed him. "John, you better come out here."

"What's the problem?" John asked, seeing Mac holding on to Otho.

"He was in there." Mac pointed to the file room. "Must have heard us."

"Otho?"

Outnumbered the young man jerked his sleeve from Mac. "Not on purpose, Sheriff. Honest."

The guilty look in Otho's eyes said otherwise, John pulled himself up to his full height, squared his shoulders, glowered down at the kid. "You want to be a lawman, you have to keep your word. Now we need your word, your solemn promise that you will tell no one, absolutely no one what you heard." He stepped closer. "Understand?"

"Yes, sir. You can trust me. I swear I'll never, ever tell."

"Alright. Now get out of here."

Bill Hawkins chuckled as Otho hurried to the door and out to the street. "Never saw anyone move so fast." He turned to his buddies. "You know he'll eventually brag to someone."

"Sure, but having the Coroner stare at him like you did just might hold him off for a while."

"I gave him my 'death' stare. That's what my kids call it when I'm after them about something."

"I better call Frank. Let him know about the body." Mac reached for his cell phone. "Probably at the Two Street Saloon in Phoenix. Be easier for her coming from him."

+ + + +

The Chief's call reached Arizona just before noon. "Frank, the bodies are at the morgue. Charlie's isn' there."

"What!"

"The Coroner is certain. We've talked to the divers and they assure us the only remains left in the pond are those of animals and - - "

"And what?"

"The remains of someone, we don't know who yet, but the body, or remains, been down there for at least fifty years, as far as the Coroner can determine. We don't know any more right now. We're trying to keep this under wraps but that won't last long and we figured you'd want to let Norma know before anyone else tells her."

"Thanks. I appreciate it.

Frank DeCani sat in his office, imagining how Norma must be feeling. He couldn't. He didn't know what it was like to have a lover turn into a murderer, stalking, planning your murder. He had to be the one to tell her, hold her in his arms, let her know he would keep her safe

He hoped the brooch he'd already sent her would tell how much he loved her.

First there were the divorces to deal with. After reserving a flight to St. Louis and assured a rental car would be waiting he called his lawyer's office. Yes, his receptionist said, he'll be in all day.

After firing his previous lawyer for lying, he'd asked friends for suggestions, someone old enough to live in the real world, with street smarts, willing to take chances for his clients. Given several names, he chose Taylor Carpenter, highly respected by judges and criminals alike, had won more cases than he'd lost, not above under-the-table deals when needed, feared by prosecutors, Frank's kind of man.

+ + + + +

The lavishly furnished law office oozed with success. Frank didn't notice, concentrating only on the words coming from the lawyer in his expensive suit, sitting behind his expensive desk saying, "My operatives made a thorough search for your wife. She's disappeared. My advice is to wait a year, get the divorce on grounds of desertion. Be patient."

Frank responded, "Bullshit!", quit the law offices of Carpenter & Carpenter, PLC with a hard jerk at the copper handle, ignoring the heavy oaken door colliding with table and lamp, glass shattering on marble flooring.

At the elevator to the parking garage a young woman and small boy waited. The elevator door opened, the woman stepped into the small enclosure, her eyes avoiding his, hands clinging protectively to the child's shoulders. Frank leaned into a corner, stayed out of her space.

Reaching the roof of the garage, long legs carried him quickly to the waiting Mercedes.

He'd always made a special effort to deal with life's problems on the straight and narrow, his small contribution to the reputation of respectable Italians. He'd never felt the deadly rage that drove people to do the unthinkable.

Until now.

The car door barely closed before anger boiled over, scarred knuckles hammered at the steering wheel. No! That bitch would not keep him from Norma. No! He stared out over the city from the top level of the parking garage for long, silent minutes. memories of Norma surging through him.

He'd made enough mistakes in his forty-eight years on this earth. He wasn't about to make another. He would do anything, everything for her. Their few kisses had opened the door to his true feelings, whetting his appetite for more.

Every night he fantasized about making love to her. He would be gentle, hold back his eagerness, crush her waiting lips with his, taste every inch of her body, feel her skin against his as they became one.

Images of waking in the morning with her sleeping peacefully beside him filled every minute of every day. Perhaps a baby, their son, would be curled between them. Norma had said she couldn't have children. He'd never wanted any, afraid of exposing them to his family's history.

He hadn't given the difference in ages any thought before. What was it? Fifteen years? She should have children. They would adopt. He'd call her, tell her again that he loves her. But say nothing about Charlie. Wait. If she doesn't say anything about him, she doesn't know yet.

He dialed the cell phone, hitting the memory button with Nell's home phone. No answer. *Norma must have a cell phone. Why the hell didn't I get the number? Doesn't Nell have one? Maybe not. I'm an idiot. Idiot!*

From the garage he drove south on Central Avenue towards Park Central Mall, open windows inviting the welcome relief of cool autumn air. Phoenix's summer had broken records, reaching 125 degrees. Like February in Chicago, cabin fever was rampant, tempers short.

The police force strained to contain the expected increase in road rage, shootings, robberies, violence, domestic, shootings, hoped for calm with lower temperatures.

The parking lot at the Mall was filled. Frank scoured the area for an empty space, driving up one aisle, down another. Spotting white back-up lights shining he cut off a car headed for the just-emptied space, taking it over at the last second..

A car screeched to a halt behind him. A man the size of a refrigerator got out. "Hey, you jerk!"

Frank answered with, "Who you calling a jerk, Tony?"

"Sorry, Frank, didn't see you through those dark windows. What the hell are you doing here - and at lunch hour?" The big man gripped Frank's shoulder. "Shouldn't you be keeping watch at Two Street?"

"Place can run by itself."   Frank shook his shoulder loose. "Have to pick something up."

"You got that hungry look and I don't mean for food. It's a woman. Am I right? Sure I'm right. I'll spring for lunch and you tell me all about her."

Frank checked his watch. "Sure. Why not? It's about time you sprung for something, considering all the free drinks my bartenders have doled out on your birthdays." They headed for the entryway to the center. "By the way, don't you think you've reached your peak of birthdays for a few years?"

"So I lie once in a while."

Benches and water fountains, white rafters enveloped in bright red bougainvillea in full bloom created a courtyard surrounded by eating places and small retailers, bookstore, a couple of jewelry stores, shoe stores, anchored by a major department store at each end.

The Phoenix Grill's outdoor patio of white tables and chairs under carnival-colored umbrellas drew a large lunch crowd from nearby high-rise office buildings.

As soon as they were seated Tony lit a cigarette and took a long, slow drag, smoke drifting slowly up around his head. "Broad won't let me smoke around her. Says she's allergic, gives her headaches. Don't want anything giving her a headache, if you get my drift."

Frank studied the thickening crowd. "How about a table with some privacy?"

"Sure. You bet." Tony waved at a waiter.

"'What can I do for you?" The young man looked anxious to please.

Tony pointed towards two women, professional types dressed in prim dark suits with white blouses, sitting at a table against a wall at the far end of the patio.

"Bet they'd enjoy the view from this table."

The waiter nodded as a ten spot found its way into his palm. "I'm sure they would, sir. Thank you."

"Thank you!"

The two men watched as the waiter bent over the women, took up their few parcels and lead them through the crowd. The two couples met halfway.

One of the women smiled at Frank. "This is very kind of you."

"Enjoy your lunch," he answered, ignoring questions in her eyes.

"They'll be wondering all day who the hell we are." Tony chuckled, as they settled in the wrought iron chairs. "Now tell me."

Tony put the cigarette out in the ashtray and lit another. "Gotta get my nicotine level up," he explained, taking a deep, lung-filling puff.

Frank sipped from the water glass as the waiter returned with menus, waiting for their order.

Tony ordered, "Cheeseburger, fries, cottage cheese, coffee, black."

"Same here." Frank grinned, "Cottage cheese?"

"Broad's got me on a diet. She asks what I had for lunch, I say cottage cheese. She's happy, I'm happy."

With the waiter out of ear-shot, Frank's grin disappeared. "I got married a year or so back."

Blowing a circle of smoke, Tony sighed. "God, I love doing that," adding "Yeah, I know. Some actress, in Vegas."

"How did you know that? Why didn't you say something?"

"First question, you forget I'm a private eye. I hear things. Second question, figured you had your reasons for keeping it quiet."

"I was an ass, that's why." Frank rearranged the cheap silverware. "Remember Gina?"

Tony only nodded.

"Caught her with some bastard musician. I took off for Vegas, got drunk as a skunk, met this gal, an actress, and to make a long story short, according to my lawyer, we got married in Vegas."

Tony started to say something but Frank held up his hand. "And in Los Angeles and in Phoenix."

"How the hell ———?"

"I was drunk and she helped me stay that way. When I sobered up, with a wife, I went to my lawyer to get out of it. He found out I'd married her three times."

"Why? What for?"

"It's funny." Frank smirked. "Enjoy yourself."

Tony swallowed the growing guffaw. "Sorry."

"Apparently I talked too much, told her about my family. She's watched the Godfather movies, I forget how many times but too damn many. She figured with DeCani in-laws, no movie producer dared turn her down, she'd get any part she wanted. Guess she hasn't done too well in her chosen career."

"DeCani is a well known name in some circles. But you're not involved any of those activities. Why'd you marry her three times?"

"Too busy drinking. Can only guess she figured I'd never be able to divorce her three times, the last time here in Phoenix before a Justice of the Peace."

Tony couldn't hold it back any longer. "Damn, what a broad!"

Frank waited patiently.

The big man choked on one last laughing spell. "So divorce her, three times if necessary."

"She's disappeared. My lawyer says he can't find her, suggests he petition the Court to make the first two marriages null and void.

"Without her, I have to claim desertion but that means waiting a year. Too long. I need to find her."

"You got somebody waiting." It wasn't a question.

"She's in Illinois. Doesn't know about this. She got hurt bad by a guy she trusted."

Tony put out the dwindling cigarette, taking his time lighting another. "Charlie Doyle."

"You know him?"

"Checked him out for a friend of yours, Mickie Mastrogiuseppe."

Frank leaned back in the chair, shaking his head. "I'll be damned."

"Why not call your cousin, PeeWee? He'll drop whatever he's got going."

Frank shook his head. "Is there anything you don't know about me?"

Tony grinned as the waiter returned, sat filled plates before them, and hurried to a customer waving for her bill.

"Not much. Your father and I had many talks at the restaurant. We were friends, like you and me. " He patted Frank's arm. "He needed someone trustworthy here in Phoenix to get things done. I filled the bill."

"Thanks. I appreciate it, Tony." Frank glanced down at the hand still on him. Tony withdrew it, tackled the cheeseburger.

Frank took the cell phone from his jacket and dialed. "Hey, Cuz. How about paying me a visit? I could use some help." He watched Tony checking out the growing lunch crowd. "Thanks, Cuz. See you in a couple of days? Great." He folded the phone, slid it back into his pocket.

Tony grinned. "Was I right"

"Sure. Said he can always use a vacation from his Chicago business." Frank ran his hand through the black hair beginning to whiten at the temples. "There's another problem. I didn't want to get PeeWee involved. Think he's worn out his welcome down in that part of Illinois."

"How so?"

They ate in silence until Frank said, "Charlie followed Norma to Illinois where she's from. He tried to kill her. So I got PeeWee to go down there, look after her. His reputation preceded him and the law liked him being there. Then Charlie killed three people, kidnapped Norma. After a scary day tracking him down, he drowned in the pond he'd planned as her burial site. In front of a lot of witnesses. Now I've learned that the divers didn't find his body. She doesn't know yet."

"You think some nut stole the body just for the hell of it?"

"Maybe. Who knows. I'm more concerned for her, how she'll feel when she hears about it. Right now the Chief of Police, he's a family friend you might say, is keeping it under wraps until I can get there."

"And you're afraid the word will get to her before you do."

"Right. It's a small town. Hard to keep a secret."

"Let me think a minute." Tony motioned to a nearby waiter. "You got any wine here?"

"Yes, sir. What would you like?"

"Surprise me, as long as it's red and none of that cheap crap."

"Yes sir."

They sat silently until the waiter returned with a carafe and two glasses.

The big man took a sip of wine. "Good stuff." He wiped his mouth, waiting until the waiter moved on.

"PeeWee's got to have contact with the phone company in that area. He can get her phone service cut off until you get there."

"He can do that?"

"Guys like him can do anything."

"What if she goes into town or somebody goes to the house?"

"You're gonna love this. How about a dangerous prisoner escapes from Joliet Federal Prison? Bulletin goes out over the state it's suspected he's headed for home in - where is she?"

"Staying with a friend outside Olney, Sailor Springs, Clay City."

"Okay, he's from Clay City. Everyone in the area is told to stay indoors until he's caught. You get back there, let PeeWee know when all is well with your girl and he'll call it off."

Frank slapped the table. "You amaze me."

Tony grinned. "Survival skills, my friend."

After lunch Tony went his way and Frank headed for the jewelry store.

The night before he'd stopped at the mall before heading home, needing to walk off the hunger for Norma building inside.

Sparkling jewelry on black velvet in the store's window had caught his eye, earrings of tiny white owls. A woman's soft drawl greeted him inside.

"Mr. DeCani, how nice to see you." She smoothed the beehive of white hair. "What can I do for you?"

"You get lovelier every time I see you, Ms. Schroeder."

"You are so like your sweet daddy. Always the gentleman."

"That's nice of you to say. He was a good man."

"Yes, he was." She slowly withdrew her hand from his. "Did the lady enjoy the brooch?"

Ignoring the question, he glanced at the glass counters. "You made some special pieces for my father."

"He had a special lady to give them to." Ms. Schroeder purred in anticipation of a big sale.

Frank led her back to the window and pointed at the earrings. "Is it possible to get those with squirrels instead of owls?"

"You wait right here."

With a saucy wink, she went behind a counter, unlocked the case, withdrew a velvet jewelry pad, and handed it to him. "I thought you'd be back."

His hand held earrings, white squirrels on black onyx. "Matching the brooch. How wonderful. Thank you."

"Are her ears pierced?"

"I don't know. Is it a problem?."

She chucked him under the chin. "No, you silly boy. These are for pierced ears but I also have the same thing in clip-ons. Always like to play it safe, especially with my favorite customers. Take these and if she wants the others I'll send them. Now, shall I gift wrap it?"

"Yes, both pairs. I like to play it safe, too. And the next time you're in the restaurant, please be my guest." He reached down and let his lips brush her cheek. "I look forward to seeing you again."

Her fingers caressed the skin his lips had touched.

Outside the shop he tried calling Norma again at Nell's. *Still no answer. She's okay. If she wasn't, someone would let me know.* He laid the phone down, still uneasy.

* * * *

At the Two Street Saloon Frank made his way through the kitchen to the back office, finding the girl from the temporary service on her knees, staring at the inner workings of the copier.

"Problem, Karen?"

"Stupid machine keeps saying there's a paper jam but I'll be damned if I can find it." She turned her pleasant, round face toward him. "Sorry, Mr. DeCani."

He laughed. "Don't apologize. I've called it worse names. I'll send in Aldo. He knows how to deal with this monster."

"Yes, sir." Karen giggled, getting to her feet.

He headed for the door. "You've been here what – two weeks now?"

"Yes sir."

"Like the job?"

She didn't hesitate. "Oh, yes, Mr. DeCani. Very much."

"Want it full time?"

At her surprised look he said "I'll take care of it with the agency."

"Thank you, Mr. DeCani. That's terrific! Thank you."

"Okay. It's done. We'll talk later about your salary."

As the door closed behind him, he heard her yell, "Wow!"

Next he headed for the kitchen. Cooks in white aprons hovered over hot grills and steaming pots. Waiters in jeans, white cowboy shirts with red-checkered neck scarves and waitresses flaunting short denim skirts with off-the-shoulder frilly white blouses kept the swinging doors moving as orders were brought in and plates of food carried out.

Busboys in jeans and tie-less white shirts hurried through with ice-cube-filled pitchers of water, clean table settings, vases of fresh flowers. He stopped one of the waiters. "You seen Aldo?"

"Too busy, Mr. D."

Frank patted him on the back. "Sorry to stop you."

He walked through the back door and stood under the purple canopy waiting for the valet tending to a customer's car. "You seen Aldo?"

The young man pointed towards a sparse grove of trees.

Frank skirted around the edge of the parking lot spotting his Chief Engineer leaning over a man on the ground. "Aldo, what's going on?"

The short, muscular man turned. "Hey, boss. This old guy and his daughter been camping out here. Customers complaining they make the place look bad. But she's got a baby and they got no place to go."

A young woman, long coal-black hair shading her face, peered out from the shadows. The whimpers of an unhappy baby grabbed at Frank's heart.

Aldo whispered, "Your dad always filled an empty belly."

Frank fished around in his pockets, finding a card he handed to Aldo. "This is a friend of mine. Take them there. She'll see they get what they need." He knelt down to the grandfather. "Habla espanol?"

The old man answered slowly and carefully.   "Si, Senor, e Ingles."

"You want a job?"

The old man grinned through few, jagged teeth. "Si, Senor!"

"What is your name?"

"Ernesto, Senor."

Frank stood up. "Aldo, any objections to Ernesto helping out around the place?" Sensing Aldo's approval, he added, "There's something else we need to talk over. Later, okay? And stop by the office. Karen's fighting with the copier."

"Whatever you say, Mr. D."

The old man's grin grew wider. "Gracias, Senor! Gracias!"

Aldo offered a hand as his new helper struggled to his feet while motioning to the girl. With the baby tight against her breast, she began gathering their belongings yet glancing towards Frank. When he bent down to help, she bowed her head and scurried after her father.

CHAPTER FOUR

The restaurant's chaotic noon rush had quieted by the time Aldo returned from delivering the trio to Mickie Mastrogiuseppe, owner of Scottsdale's illustrious restaurant and salon, Villa de Rosa. A long time friend of Louie DeCani's, Mickie could always be counted on.

Frank waved to him from a corner booth. With cold beers before them, Frank said, "You do a good job of running this place whether I'm here or not and I appreciate it, Aldo."

"Thanks, Mr. D."

"I'm going to be gone for awhile, a long while. You run the place?

"Sure. Trouble?"

"No. I just need to be in Illinois, to take care of some personal business."

"Norma?"

Frank studied the man's rugged face. Aldo's years as a professional boxer showed in the broken nose, the ears too big for his head. Aldo had access to everything at the restaurant, knew every inch of it, how it all worked. A quiet man, he saw and heard things shared only with the boss when needed.

Louie DeCani had trusted the tough guy. So could his son. Frank nodded.

Sitting in the same booth he and his father had sat with Norma and her husband brought back bittersweet memories. He'd watched the two of them, always touching, exchanging smiles.

Those were the times he thought of having a wife, of sharing love secrets, someone to be happy with, to love and to hold.

Now Jack was gone. Norma needed a strong man to love her, care for her, make her happy. He'd finally allowed himself to admit how much he loved her, not as just a friend. No, much more than that.

He would build a new life with her. Now that Charlie was dead the danger was over. There was no reason he couldn't be with Norma, help her in raising money for restoring her beloved hometown, Sailor Springs, Illinois.

His wife would be found. She would give him a divorce.

First he needed reassurance. Not that he didn't trust Tony to be straight with him. But he couldn't afford any mistakes. He leaned closer to Aldo. "You're the one man my father trusted, depended on."

Aldo sipped his coffee, rubbed at a spot on the table with the ever-present bar towel. "Trusted me with his life. So can you, Mr. D."

"Then tell me. Was my father's life ever threatened?"

"Because of Bugsy?"

Frank nodded.

Aldo studied the man before him, the man Louie DeCani had left to care for the restaurant he'd loved, to keep his promise to the employees they would always have a job there, be taken care of, and if in trouble he was ready to help.

"One night two guys got past his security system at the house. Louie woke up with a gun stuck between his eyes. Didn't say a word, just stood there, then left. He understood their message Any time, any place."

"And?"

"The word on the street was a contract on his life. Big money. A million. Few days later cops found a couple thugs in the desert - dead. Mob style, they said. No more threats." Aldo finished his coffee and went back behind the bar.

CHAPTER FIVE

That night, as with every night, Frank DeCani sat in his favorite recliner in the den of his father's house and reviewed events of the day while sipping on a double shot of Chivas Regal.

Louie DeCani had little formal education but he'd taught himself from books and experiences, his photographic memory retaining it all. The walk-in closet remained lined with books floor to ceiling, wall to wall.

Frank gazed at the picture above the fireplace, Louie and Theresa on their wedding day, the bride tall, slim, with dark hair flowing over her shoulders, large eyes filled with expectations. And Louie, handsome in his black tuxedo, dark wavy hair, smiling proudly at his beautiful bride

Aunt Rosie had told him many times that it was a beautiful wedding, how happy they were when she became pregnant soon after the honeymoon.

Frank took a bigger sip of the strong liquid.

His mind pushed aside the business of the day, bringing forth the night at Aunt Rosie's, sitting on the couch where she'd often calmed his childhood fears, and told how life changed when Louie went to work in Las Vegas. Her words remained etched in his brain.

Louie had refused to have Theresa and the baby join him. Theresa begged, pleaded that a family should be together. All to no avail. One night she went out, leaving the baby with Aunt Rosie, and was never heard from again.

Frank stared long and hard into the silent eyes of his mother's face. The little boy inside never stopped hoping she would come back to him.

He forced his mind to the present day. What a bitch of a day. Aldo would take care of business. Maybe he'd make him a partner.

He glanced at the wall clock. Was Illinois one or two hours ahead of Arizona? In any event, too late to try calling Norma again.

+ + + + +

Before the sun showed itself the next morning, Frank's phone rang. "Hello?"

"Okay, Cuz. I'm here."

"PeeWee? You're in Phoenix?"

"If you'll open your door –"

Frank yanked up his briefs while holding the portable phone under his chin, stumbled over the book he'd dropped to the floor when falling asleep the night before. "Damn!" Limping to the front door he heard from the phone "Back door!"

Forcing his mind to function, he made his way down the hall and through the kitchen, glanced through the one-way mirrored door before unlocking the security screen.

The little man in his usual black suit sauntered inside. "Hey, Cuz. How the hell are ya?"

"Get the hell in here." Frank growled, grasping his throbbing big toe. "Didn't expect you so soon."

"You need me, I'm here. Got any coffee?"

"Make it yourself."

Frank pulled a can of coffee from the cupboard, pointed at the coffee pot and left to take a quick shower.

That done, the cousins settled in the den.

PeeWee took his suit coat off and laid it carefully across the back of the nearby sofa. Frank flinched at the size of the gun in his shoulder holster. PeeWee pushed it further back but didn't remove it.

Frank gave a shortened version of his marriages.

PeeWee seemed to concentrate only on the coffee.

"Got yourself in quite a jam."

Frank knew he'd absorbed, deciphered every word. His five foot cousin in size six shoes survived by seeing and hearing things other people missed, revealing nothing, retaining power over those bigger and stronger, those who gave him power in return for what he didn't tell.

"I need you to find my," Frank choked on the word, "wife."

"Name?"

"Dawn Dupree, now DeCani."

"Hard to say, huh?"

"A bitch."

"I'll find her. Do I need to know why?"

Frank told what he knew about Charlie's missing body, stressing that he had to be the one to tell Norma.

Frank measured his next words, "Norma is still at Nell's. I don't want her finding out any of this from anyone but me. Can you get her phone service cut off for a short time?"

"No problem, Cuz."

"Have to keep anyone from getting out to Nell's, too."

"Got any ideas how I'm to do that?"

"Maybe. Say a psychopathic killer escapes from Joliet Federal Prison, wouldn't authorities all over the state be alerted, maybe they suspect he's headed home, downstate?"

"Cuz, you surprise the hell out of me. Either you been talkin' to someone or you're gettin' dangerous in your old age."

"Cut it out. A friend suggested it."

"Good friend to have, if you ask me." PeeWee slicked back his coal black hair still worn in the ducktail style of years long gone, caught sight of the photo on the wall. "Uncle Louie and Aunt Theresa. Good lookin' couple."

Frank ignored the compliment. "You hungry?"

"Yeah. What ya got?"

"Eggs and bacon okay?"

"Nothin' fancy, okay? I know ya like cookin' gourmet style but I'm for just plain old sunny-side up eggs, crispy bacon, and maybe some toast and jelly, grape, if ya got it."

"Come on, Cuz. I'll make you a breakfast you'll never forget."

"Oh, cripe." PeeWee imagined eggs he wouldn't recognize.

Frank pulled him from his chair, followed by a playful push down the hall to the kitchen.

The spacious room was the same as Louie had fashioned it, red brick floor, pink stove with copper hood. Though garish and out-of-date, memories of father and son cooking together, judging each other's sauce, trying new pasta dishes, getting tipsy on Chianti filled the air. They were cherished memories.

He hadn't seen much of his father when he was growing up. Aunt Rosie had explained many times to the young boy that his father loved him very much, would always make certain he had the best of everything, but Las Vegas wasn't a place for children.

While Frank cracked eggs, tempting PeeWee with the smell of thin bacon strips sizzling in a pan, he was brought up-to-date on family affairs.

"Ma's the same, feisty, bossy. Little Mary still smokin'. Doc keeps tellin' her to quit, it's gonna kill her but she's *capatost*, head like a rock."

Popping bread in the toaster, Frank laughed. "The whole family is *capatost*."

"Hey, don't knock it, Cuz. Got me where I am."

"Good enough?" Frank slid a filled plate at PeeWee who eyed it carefully.

"Eggs with lacy edges, bacon crispy, toast perfect. Where's the jelly?"

Frank put a jar in front of him. "Happy now?"

"It'll do."

"Just eat." After allowing a few moments to enjoy the hot food and PeeWee had lit his after-breakfast cigarette, Frank made his next request. "Hope I'm not asking too much but need another favor."

The little man leaned back in his chair, a contented look on his scrawny face. "Shoot."

"I want the divorce ASAP. The private eye, the one that tried to hire you when Bard was looking for Charlie, he's an expert on the computer. Bard says he can find anyone with it." He watched PeeWee closely, detecting resistance.

"I know you can do the job without help, Cuz, but it will be faster this way. Larry, that's the guy, he can speed things up."

"You really got the hots for this dame, don't ya?"

Frank glared back. "He lives in Vegas. Yes or no?"

PeeWee shrugged his narrow shoulders. "Ok, Cuz. Whatever ya want. But ———-"

"What?"

"He gives me any lip, I'm out."

"He won't. Bard knows him, trusts him. That's enough."

"College boys. You always stick together."

Frank relaxed. "I'll ask Bard to let Larry know you're coming. You hear anything about Norma?"

"Remember Vito, he owns the restaurant in Olney?"

"Sure. Great food."

"Vito's wife ran into her the other day. Norma's working on a story her grandmother wrote but didn't finish. And she got involved with the group trying to rebuild that town, Sailor Springs. Some strange things been happening."

Frank leaned forward. "Like?"

"There was a fire at one of the houses they wanted to restore. It got spotted before too much damage was done, another one at the Town Hall, in the kitchen, next to the storage room where a lot of the town's records were kept. Just by luck they'd been taken out the night before for some committee to look over."

The room became very still. Frank studied his scarred knuckles. "Kids?"

"Don't know. Sheriff's looking into it." PeeWee stood up, yawning. "I gotta get some shuteye." "Where do I crash?"

Frank reached for the phone. "Take the guest room down the hall on the left. I'll be leaving early so sleep in, help yourself to whatever you need. Call me after you talk to Larry."

"Gotcha."

CHAPTER SIX

Frank's usual morning routine included a run down the horse path on Central Avenue, through the neighborhood of stately old homes, around the block and back home to down a super-powered drink of something he couldn't pronounce but a customer big on health highly recommended.

This morning a quick shave and shower sufficed. He dressed in one of many Italian-made suits hanging in his closet, choosing to accompany it a white shirt, silk tie with matching pocket handkerchief.

While packing his suitcase, he dialed Nell's number reaching a recording of, "This number has been temporarily disconnected. Please try your call again."

At the restaurant he asked Karen to show him how to bring up a Chicago newspaper on the computer, then go next door to Jordan's Mexican Restaurant and get him a couple of beef tacos, chips and hot dip. And whatever she'd like, too.

She grimaced at the idea of such a breakfast but did as he asked.

As soon as the door closed behind her, he turned to the computer screen, found the search icon, typed in "Joliet, Illinois". Within seconds there it was, column headed in bold, reading, "Dangerous Criminal Escapes Joliet State Prison."

The article described horrific murders the escapee had committed, told that authorities believed he was headed downstate, towards Clay County where a sister lived on a farm. Warnings were out to travelers, residents were asked to be out on the roads only in an emergency. PeeWee must have made some calls from the bedroom.

Frank hit the 'back' icon, returning the screen to the computer's desktop. Time for Aldo to drive him to the airport.

CHAPTER SEVEN

While Aldo headed the Mercedes onto Squaw Peak Parkway towards the airport, Frank didn't watch the construction of a new freeway connecting the valley's east and west sides, the high-rises of Phoenix's center, the heavy traffic hurrying past.

His mind saw only the wide countryside of Illinois with its fields of corn and soybeans, Norma waiting for him at Nell's farmhouse.

At the terminal, Frank pulled his one suitcase from the back seat, reminded Aldo to help Karen with the copier, waved goodbye, and turned to face whatever the future held.

As usual the airport teemed with the noise of people hurrying this way and that, scouring for directions, children crying, adults scanning TV screens for departures, arrivals, dogs barking from their crates, businessmen with attaché cases and laptop computers, teenagers laden with bulging backpacks.

Frank ignored it all, looking for a somewhat quiet corner. Finally he gave up, turned his back to the chaos and called Chief MacLoone's office.

The Chief's daughter told him her father was out but she could find him, if needed. He said no, that was okay, he'd see him in a day or so.

The next three and a half hours to St. Louis International Airport gave Frank time to reflect on his life, what it had been, how he wanted his future.

He'd done what his father wanted, graduated from college with a Bachelors Degree in business while he secretly yearned to be head chef of a renowned restaurant.

When Louie died he continued being the good son and kept Two Street Saloon as his father wished.

Then the woman he loved crushed his heart and he went off the deep end, marrying a stupid broad not once but three times. He'd be kicking himself forever.

Now there was Norma. His life had to change.

At St. Louis the sudden loud thud of tires hitting the tarmac shook him back to reality. Slowly, agonizingly slow, the plane inched towards the terminal.

It took every ounce of restraint he could muster to keep from crawling over the seats, past the crush of passengers struggling with bags and suitcases, and forcing the door open.

He waited impatiently as the plane unloaded, made his way through the passageway, escaped the crowd, hurried downstairs to the car rental desk.

The line moved quickly, the sedan he'd requested waited curbside.

He was on his way to Illinois and Norma.

On Route 50, he pushed the car above the speed limit into Illinois, past bleak fields waiting for the coming winter, remembering Norma's hair in the sunlight, glowing like the red sky of a tropical sunset. Someday he would take her to Hawaii and show her such a sunset.

He wanted to call her, hear her voice but knew it would be futile. No calls would get through to her until he called PeeWee.

Ninety minutes later he spotted the Clay City sign.

His mind hinted at the smell of her perfume, always of flowers. He would buy her flowers, lots of flowers, flowers of all kinds, of all colors. He would surround her with flowers.

A siren's wail interrupted his thoughts. The rear view mirror showed a black SUV, lights flashing, bearing down on him.

He slowed the car, pulling off the road, and stopped.

Lowering the window he saw Sheriff Brawley in uniform.

"Hello, John."

"Hi yourself, Frank."

"Norma okay?"

"I was just on my way to Nell's. Her phone's been out and we got a fugitive on the loose. Couldn't raise her on her cell either. That happens a lot around here."

Using the face that had bluffed many a poker hand, Frank asked, "This guy dangerous?"

"Afraid so. We've warned every one to stay in til he's caught. Escaped from Joliet Pen, got kinfolk around here. Saw this car with rental plates, figured you'd be a stranger, didn't know what was going on."

"Thanks, John. I'm sure Norma's okay. Between the dogs and those geese Nell keeps I don't think anyone gets near her place without being spotted. Have you found Charlie's body yet?"

"No. Maybe some kids took him just for hell of it. Some of them are amateur scuba divers. Wouldn't be surprised. Years ago someone stole a body from a crypt out at the White Cemetery. Not much else for them to do around here."

"You're probably right.   Norma doesn't know yet?"

"I don't think so."

Frank put the car in gear. "It'll be dark soon, John."

Sheriff John Brawly backed away from the car, grinning. "Sure, Frank. Know Norma'll be glad to see you."

Frank waited until the Sheriff drove off before heading on to Nell's place, past fields now gone to seed, some still holding oil wells, some lying idle, others pulling the thick, black riches from underground. Fading in the twilight, white oil tanks waited in the fields.

Another few minutes and he turned onto the narrow lane leading to the house. Gripping the steering wheel with sweaty palms, he eased the car forward, wondering what to expect when he told her about Charlie's missing body.

The farmhouse with the wrap-around porch appeared freshly painted, white with green shutters and trim. He stopped at the closed gate.

Nell's two dogs rushed forward from the other side, first with harsh warning barks quickly changing to great yelps and leaps into the air at the familiar scent.

There was movement from the porch, Norma cautiously crossing the lawn.

Frank stepped out of the car and waved. He sighed in relief as she opened the gate and ran into his arms.

"Hi." She murmured as his lips met hers.

Frank grinned down at this woman who had his heart. "Let's get the car inside."

"I'll close the gate."

With the dogs at her side, she locked the gate.

While he parked the car she waited by the back door, calling out, "Want some coffee?"

"Is there any of that last bottle of wine I bought before I left or did you and Nell drink it all?"

"No." She held the screen door open. "I'll get it. Where's your luggage or aren't you staying?"

"I'll find something in town. Wanted to see you first." He leaned against the kitchen counter, watching her take wine from the refrigerator, glasses from the cabinet. "Where's Nell?"

"Visiting a sick friend. When I got back from a walk there was a note the phone is out, said she'd call me later.

"Where's your cell?"

"Upstairs. Haven't used it for awhile."

"You're alone out here?"

"I don't mind." She handed him the wine bottle. "Do the honors?"

"Sure."

"Let's go in the sun room."

He followed her through French doors onto a porch surrounded by glass panels curving down from the roof to the floor. Two small round tables covered with white linen, a couch, and a scattering of chairs along with thriving potted plants made for pleasant surroundings. He took the glasses and the bottle from her, set them down on one of the tables. "I have to tell you something."

Norma kept silent, watching him closely.

Frank stifled the urge to hold her. "This is going to sound crazy but here goes. You know the - - the bodies were retrieved from Soft Pond?"

"Yes."

"Charlie's wasn't there."

Her eyes narrowed. "How did you know?"
"The Sheriff. Said he'd try to keep it quiet until I got here. Who told you?"

"Betty, waitress at the café in Olney. She drove out."

"But I thought there was a convict on the loose, everyone was supposed to stay off the roads."

"She couldn't wait. Said she thought I needed to know."

"Thoughtless, if you ask me".

"Betty's always been a tail." She reached for the wine, sipping it slowly. "He's dead. We all saw him." A shiver ran through her at the memory. "Divers probably just missed him. Dark, muddy at the bottom."

He motioned towards the couch. "She's been a what?"

The soft cushions drew her into their nest "A tail. It's a local thing. I'm trying to be a lady."

"And that you are, Lady Guinevere."

"And you, Sir Lancelot, are a gentleman."

Their glasses clinked, eyes meeting.

"Did you think I'd forget you were Guinevere in King Arthur's Court while your little friends played Roy Rogers, chasing bank robbers."

"Back when life was simple, when blossoms of hollyhocks became ballerinas, corncobs changed into dolls in disguise, baby chicks had names, and cats dressed in doll clothes for fancy tea parties."

"You said Sailor Springs was full of magic and wonder."

"To a child it was."

"I missed you."

With legs tucked under, fingers wrapped around the wine glass, she appeared so small, fragile. Spying him from the yard she'd rushed to him. Now an unspoken barrier had risen between them. "What's the price these days?"

"Huh?"

"You know, a penny for your thoughts, inflation, all that."

"Of course. Let's see." Tiny wrinkles appeared on her forehead. "Taking into consideration time and labor, more than anyone would want to pay."

"Try me." Tantalized by the scent of flowers flowing from her he leaned forward. "Please."

Time seemed to stop as Norma sat gazing at him.

He stood up. "I'll be right back."

She heard the screen door snap shut behind him. A car door opened, closed. The man now coming back into the house had cared for her, whisked her away from Charlie's reach, kept her safe. She'd trusted Charlie, and had been so wrong, so dangerously wrong. Could she, should she trust again?

The times she and Charlie had been together still haunted her, his face as she left him in Phoenix, walking towards the plane to Utah, so lonely, forlorn. The urge to run back to him, tell him she'd never leave him was overwhelming. Still she'd managed to turn away.

His E-mails, his lovemaking, all described how desperate he was to have her with him at all costs. Yet overnight he'd changed into a maniac, stalking her, killing innocent people.

Only because of his wife's warning of his mental illness did she believe anyone could change from a loving, caring person into such a monster. He'd deceived her completely.

The first time Frank kissed her, his lips touched hers softly, hesitating only a second before pressing on, holding his lips to hers briefly, enough to take her breath away.

And the day Charlie died in the pond Frank spent the night with her. All through the dark hours he hadn't spoken a word, unconditionally giving the protection of his love, holding her gently against him, through the sobbing, the pain until she fell mercifully asleep. Still part of her held back from the love he offered.

She watched the doorway, waiting, wondering whether to ask him to stay the night. At the sound of his footsteps coming closer she shoved aside such thoughts.

Frank offered a ribboned box.

She took it, carefully slipped off the ribbon, slowly raising the lid. "Oh, Frank. You didn't."

"Looks like I did." He grinned. "Do you like them?"

Gingerly she held up the earrings. "They are lovely. Thank you." She raised her eyes to his. "I loved the brooch, too. I - I just can't - - ."

He sat down, hesitantly, fighting back the passion surging through him. "Too soon?"

"Yes," her voice so low he barely heard her.

He moved closer.

She said nothing more, as though waiting. For what, he wondered, daring to touch her arm, feeling the slightest movement towards him.

His lips close to hers, he whispered, "Let me love you, sweetheart."

Her breathing deepened. The almost forgotten quickening deep within spread, giving life to hunger long ignored. He held her face close to his, drowning in the green eyes flecked with gold. "Only what you want. Nothing more."

Tomorrow he would visit Sheriff Brawley and Chief MacLoone. Tonight he wanted only to love the woman in his arms.

CHAPTER EIGHT

While dawn rose over the quiet countryside, Frank forbid his eyes to open, enjoying the feel of his love's naked body curled in arms savoring fulfillment.

Slowly she stirred, rolled over to face him. "Hi."

"Morning, glory."

She touched a finger to his lips. "You're starting to sound like the folks around here."

"Not a bad place to be."

"Hmmmmm," she purred, kissing his chest.

Afraid of ruining the moment, he hesitated to ask but instinct warned there was more she wasn't telling. "There's something bothering you. What is it?"

She stiffened, pulling away. "It's Charlie - Nell saw him."

"What?" he sat up.

"The day before the - the bodies were taken from the pond."

"My God, Norma. How could she even think that?"

Punching her pillow into a comfortable lump she scooted up beside him. "She wouldn't lie to me. If it wasn't Charlie, it was his twin."

"There wasn't a twin. Bard would have told me."

"Nell said she was driving into town and he passed her on a motorcycle. She just got a glance, couldn't see his face clearly, had on goggles but no mistaking the hair."

"Someone must be playing a rotten joke on the both of you. Whoever it is I will personally - - -."

"Why would anyone do that?"

"Who knows. But we'll find out. I promise."

"You're right. I shouldn't be upset."

"Maybe somebody's got a grudge against you or maybe her. Maybe there's a joker in Sailor Springs who is just plain bored."

An impish grin appeared on Norma's face.

He laughed. "A story brewing in that mind?"

"That's what I do, remember?"

"Damn, you're not only beautiful and adorable, but smart."

"Thank you, Sir Lancelot. Now how about I go downstairs and make us some coffee?"

"Not yet," he whispered, drawing her down to him.

CHAPTER NINE

PeeWee cruised through the development just south of Las Vegas, it's streets wide with golf cart lanes along the curbs. Houses of stucco and brick sat far back on wide lots, patios facing a six-foot wall muffling sounds of heavy traffic on the other side.

Used to the narrow streets of Chicago, a constant kaleidoscope of moving colors and sounds on the narrow streets, he wondered at the silence. The street was empty of cars, people, not even the noise of a barking dog.

Checking the address on his notepad, he spotted #14392 painted in white on the curb.

As he drove onto the flower-lined driveway, a young man waved from a wheelchair.

PeeWee deliberately took his time getting out of the car, ambled slowly up the sidewalk, checking out the surroundings.

The house was much like its neighbors, neatly trimmed shrubs framing the walkway, white pebbles encircling tall cacti, large exotic plants on each side of the front door.

"Hello, Mr. DeCani." The young man smiled, holding out his hand, the knuckles gnarled by the arthritis, fingers bent unnaturally.

PeeWee took it, being careful to put little pressure.

Frank had briefed him on Larry, intelligent, confident, expert at finding anything or anyone over the Internet. Confined to a wheelchair by rheumatoid arthritis since the age of fifteen hadn't stopped him from traveling the world.

He'd worked part-time for a private investigator firm until the boss took a special interest in him and feeling Larry was a natural, suggested he go into business for himself, offering his assistance and using his license as an apprentice. Bard Bolden Doyle was his only client until now and he did well investing in the stock market over the Internet.

"You Larry?"

He nodded, "Come on in, Mr. DeCani."

"PeeWee. Just call me PeeWee."

Larry spun the wheelchair around and headed down a hallway. "Right this way, PeeWee."

Peewee followed, glancing at rooms on each side of the wide hallway, instinctively memorizing smells, sounds, furnishings. His neck muscles relaxed; his attention shifted to the young man expertly navigating the electric chair around a corner.

Larry looked to be in his early thirties, long limbs, a good-looking man, with sandy-colored hair that held a deep wave from the broad forehead down to his shoulders. PeeWee didn't much like long hair on a man but Larry carried it off.

"Sit anywhere," Larry stopped, locking the wheelchair in place, seemingly unimpressed with a member of
the DeCani family now sitting in his house, in his office,
expecting his help, black suit most likely covering a gun
in a shoulder holster.

His guest pulled out a cigarette. Larry frowned.
"I'd prefer you not smoke in here. Sensitive electronics."

PeeWee slipped the cigarette back in the pack.
Kid wasn't afraid of him. He liked that.

His eyes scanned the room filled with computers,
printers, Fax machines, a complicated looking phone set,
and what looked like a mini-lab.

Filing cabinets lined one side of the room, the
remaining walls holding large windows giving a broad
view of the front, side, and back of the house. PeeWee
thought from the looks of them they were all one-way
mirrors.

He didn't spot Larry's hand slipping under the
wheelchair.

Steel shields slammed down from the ceiling,
enveloping the windows. PeeWee jumped from his chair.
"Holy shit!"

"The house is now bullet proof."

"Holy shit!"

The young man grinned. "Forgive me. I don't get
many chances to show off my toys." He pushed the
button under his chair again; the shields quietly returned
to their hiding places above.

Larry faced PeeWee. "Let's get one thing clear. Despite the need for this," he patted the chair, "I can go anywhere, do anything I want so don't for one minute think of me as handicapped. I have my limitations but don't we all?"

PeeWee arched an eyebrow at the brash young man. "You gotta lotta nerve. I like that"

"Shall I ask my wife to bring some refreshments?"

PeeWee's eyebrows arched.

"I'm still a man, PeeWee." He called out, "Maria. May we have ——— "he stopped and nodded to PeeWee who shrugged, "Whatever."

"Coffee, and maybe some of those Biscotti?"

A voice from somewhere in the house answered, "Right away."

PeeWee detected a slight Italian accent

Larry got his attention back with, "Bard said your cousin needs help. What can I do?"

As PeeWee told about Frank's wife and the marriages his eyes kept flicking back to the doorway. After a few moments light footsteps were heard.

"Here we are." Bright dark eyes met PeeWee's stare. "Hello. I'm Maria. You are Mr. DeCani."

"PeeWee. Just call me PeeWee."

He couldn't hide his admiration for her slim figure lesser women would die for and hair so black as to be almost blue, large dark eyes, full of mischief. "Southern Italy?"

She smiled as she sat the tray down. "You are definitely Italiano. Yes, my parents are from Sicily."

PeeWee turned to Larry. "Lucky man."

Maria kissed her husband's cheek. "I am the lucky one. Now I will leave you alone."

"Thank you, Maria." Larry enjoyed PeeWee's obvious interest as Maria disappeared down the hall. "Shall we get down to business?"

"How do you figure we can help each other?" PeeWee reached for the Biscotti, dropping it as the computer flashed a picture of him followed by his file from the Chicago Police Department along with his family's history.

"How the hell ———— ?" PeeWee watched as Larry scrolled down, bringing more information to the screen. "Where you get this stuff?"

"By getting in where I'm not supposed to. That's what I can do for you." Larry added, "Pal."

PeeWee roared. "You got that in there too?"

"Sure. That's your trademark, calling everyone *pal* ."

"I'll be damned." PeeWee leaped out of the way as Larry spun the wheelchair around.

"Here's the deal. I'm the expert on cyberspace, the Internet, a nerd, if you will. You have the street smarts. With the computer I can get in places you can't but you can go where I can't. People notice a man in a wheel-chair."

"What is this going to cost me?"

"Your friendship."

PeeWee took in the young man's gnarled hands, his legs covered by the brightly colored afghan, neck slightly bent causing him to always be looking up, sometimes twinkling, sometimes not. He understood the need for a friend like him. "You work for Bard Bolden?"

Cautious eyes met PeeWee's. "Yes."

"What do you do for him?"

"None of your business."

"Okay. But I don't know a damn thing about you except you live in a wheelchair and you got a doll of a wife. You know about me. Your turn."

Larry pointed to licenses, certificates on the wall. "Good enough?"

PeeWee dismissed the credentials with a wave of his hand..

"Follow me." Larry spun the wheelchair around again, led PeeWee through a breezeway to the garage. There sat a strange-looking contraption.

PeeWee stared. "What in the hell is that?"

"An outdoor all-terrain electric wheelchair. I call it my funny car." Larry patted it affectionately.

"It will take me almost anywhere, through sand, gravel, over river rocks, on snow, ice, even through a foot of water. Has headlights, taillights, air cooling, a heater, a stereo. Comes with two tops, soft and hard and can be used in any kind of weather. Has a couple of James Bond-type accessories also."

He pointed under the console. "I can release a smoke screen, let go with a miniature Aldo gun. There's a loud speaker, infra-red lights for nighttime, and a two-way radio activated from the moment the ignition switch is turned on."

"Holy shit!" PeeWee walked around the thing, sliding his hand over its gleaming surface. "I never seen anything like this before."

Larry laughed. "The basic model is on the market but not widely used. It's pretty expensive for every day use. I don't get to use it much but I like to play with it."

"Gotta tell ya, I'm impressed."

"Go ahead. Get in. Just lift up on the side guards."

PeeWee slid onto the cushioned seat and took hold of the joy stick. "How fast does this baby go?"

"Normal speed is 6 mph but this has been modified to do 10. Any more and there's danger of losing control." Larry headed out the door. "Come on, partner."

Grudgingly PeeWee left the 'funny car' and followed Larry out a side door onto a path lined with brightly colored snapdragons leading around to the back of the house where another surprise waited.

There the path split, one branch leading to a covered patio of potted flowers and cushioned furniture, the other winding through a garden of raised platforms.

Mesh screens shielded vegetables ready for the picking; lettuce, cucumbers, tomatoes, kale, onions, green beans. Larry picked a handful of cheery tomatoes he handed to PeeWee.

"You grow all this in the desert?"asked PeeWee savoring each bite.

"My wife. She loves fresh vegetables. I swear she can grow anything anywhere."

"My mother's the same way. We live in an apartment on the second floor. She has a garden on the roof. No where else to plant anything in the middle of Chicago. Grows the sweetest tomatoes you ever put in your mouth –," he winked, "east of Nevada."

CHAPTER TEN

Norma gazed out the kitchen window, past trees and flowers, across open fields. She hadn't felt so awake, so aware, so alive since Jack's death. She'd been asleep for all those years until Charlie woke her with his unreal passion.

Frank was different. He was real. Upstairs in her bed he'd touched a place deep within, continued touching until she emptied of all past experiences, filled only with him.

Her skin savored his touch, his hands gently, slowing discovering her body and quickly withdrawing from the places of past hurts, his kiss passionate yet undemanding. He'd explored every inch of her until her breath came in quick gasps, and she was his.

She pushed the white organdy curtains aside and rising up on tiptoe stretched her arms skyward, her renewed body rejoicing in the moment.

Arms encircled her waist and a voice whispered, "Happy, sunshine?"

"Mmmmm," she sighed. "Very."

"What are you thinking?" He kissed her hair, taking in its delightful scent.

"Nothing. Absolutely nothing."

"Good."

They stood quietly together, taking in the sounds of country living coming to life, drifting through the window birds playing in the branches of a nearby tree, an unseen rooster crowing. From somewhere a cow mooed and another answered.

Tell her now, an inner voice jabbed at Frank's mind. He pushed the thought away. He wouldn't, couldn't risk losing her.

The serene moment broke as Nell's truck pulled up to the gate, the dogs barked, geese honked, and the phone rang. Norma tore herself out of his arms and ran for the gate while Frank grabbed the phone.

"Hey, PeeWee. How are things in Nevada?"

"Not so good, Cuz. Larry keeps saying we'll find her but I got doubts. She's really dug herself a deep hole."

Through the kitchen window and past the window box of petite lemon yellow mums Frank watched Norma swing the gate open.

He still felt her feverish body giving itself to him willingly and completely. He would have her beside him forever, no matter what it took.

"Just find her." Frank's voice dropped until barely audible. He tore away from the window. "Find her."

"There's something else, Frankie. Larry's mother is a close friend of Norma's. Name's Carol Sims.

"You sure?"

"Yeah. Larry told me, said his mom wanted a guy named Charlie Doyle checked out. He was causing a good friend of hers some trouble. Norma's the friend. Also, his mom is a retired deputy sheriff from Utah."

"What did he find out about Charlie?"

"Not much. Former stockbroker. Paid his taxes, voted in all the elections. No criminal record. Took early retirement for health reasons. Under a head doctor's care,weekly counseling sessions. Neighbors said he cheated on his wife, even beat her but she sticks with him. Good family man - on the surface. And — ."

"What?"

"Larry's old man asked him to look up Charlie Doyle too, though he used the name Chuck Bolden. Said it was for a friend. Wouldn't tell Larry who it was. Or at least that's what he's tellin' me."

"Strange," muttered Frank. "Try again?"

"Sure, Cuz. But kid's got ethics."

"Thanks, PeeWee."

"No problema."

The noise of Nell's truck wiped away Frank's frown. He took the cup of coffee out onto the narrow back steps.

Nell, dressed in blue jeans, a man's plaid shirt, and wide-brimmed straw hat, arms holding snapdragons and mums, playfully pushed the dogs aside. "As Grandma Prosser used to call to the town's children - Morning, Glory!"

"Good morning to you. What have you got there?"
Frank followed Nell into the mud room at the edge of the
kitchen.

Inside she spread the fresh flowers out on the
workbench. "Gifts from my patient." She turned, her
arms open wide. "Give me a hug, you scamp."

"What did I do?"

"Let's just say nobody around here worried about
Norma being alone last night."

"Sheriff's got a big mouth."

"Few secrets around here." She winked, giving
him a playful nudge.

From the back yard Norma yelled, "Come on you
two. It's too grand a day to be inside. Frank, would you
bring some coffee?"

"Go on now. I'll be out in a minute." Nell began
separating the flowers, hands callused from years of hard
farm work revealing her gentle soul as she carefully
placed one against the other.

With coffee pot in one hand and cups hanging
from fingers on the other, Frank nudged the screen door
open with his foot.

He stopped, watching as Norma scratched the dogs
ears, sliding her hand over their smooth backs. She
turned, smiling up at him.

He let the door close and handed her one of the
cups. "Shall we have coffee on the swing, Lady
Guinevere?"

"If you so desire, my lord." She placed the other
on his forearm and strolled towards the swing with her
Sir Lancelot.

Nell joined them much too soon. "Okay, you two. Now what happens?"

The smile vanished from Frank's face. "First I want to know about Charlie."

Nell's eyes held Frank's. "I thought I saw him. Must have been mistaken." She turned to Norma. "I shouldn't have told you."

"I know. It's okay." Nerves twitching at any mention of Charlie, Norma said, "Now tell us about Bard."

Nell's weathered face glowed. "That crazy man says he wants to court me. Can you imagine? Big city boy and plain country bumpkin. Amazing."

Norma laughed. "Frank here is the city boy, Nell. You forget Bard is from Sailor Springs, just like us."

"I just can't get over this happening. After my husband died, I thought romance, love, marriage had ended for me."

"So when is the wedding?" He stole a look at Norma. Saw no clue to her thoughts.

"You're jumping the gun, Frank." She looked up at the house she loved. "Like the new paint job? I wanted it done before he came back."

"It's great, Nell. Norma tells me there's been some trouble in town."

"Afraid so. Nothing serious, so far. A couple of fires. Sheriff says it's probably just kids but we're afraid it's more than that. Some people who don't want the town changed."

"How is Tom Crockett doing about getting a State Grant to help out?" His hand slid across the table to Norma's.

"Tom feels certain we'll get a small one to put in a water system. The town's never had that."

"It's a start. Anything else getting done?"

"Yes. Would you like a tour?" Norma loved the autumn, with its bright foliage, a nip in the air, holding back winter, perfect time for a long, slow walk.

"I'd love it. But first I have some phone calls to make and visit with Mac."

Both women stared at him. Norma asked, "Why the Chief of Police?"

"Maybe I can find out more about the fires, see if he has any clues." He grinned at them. "Don't want your town becoming a poke-or-plumb town."

"A what?"

"Poke your head out as you drive through or you'll plumb miss it. Just something my dad picked up from a friend from Kentucky ."

Nell laughed. "Those country sayings'll get to you."

"I'll come with you." Norma stood up. "But first we need breakfast. Ham and eggs anyone?"

"Sounds great but I need to see Mac - alone. You mind?"

Though Norma's eyes told him differently, she smiled, "No, of course not. I have plenty to do here. Let's eat," and went inside the house.

Nell's hand on Frank's arm held him back.

Whispering she said, "I know what I saw."

He shook his head towards Norma. Nell acknowledged his silent meaning with a nod. No more would be said - unless necessary.

CHAPTER ELEVEN

Driving alone gave Frank time to think. *It isn't supposed to be this way. Charlie's dead. I saw him die. Norma needs to forget about him. How can she with some son-of-a-bitch running around making people think he's back? I want him out of our lives.*

At the Olney Police Station the young woman at the desk behind the security doors buzzed him in without asking for identification. *One of the perks of a small town. Everyone knows you.* The Chief's office door opened.

"Mac."

"Frank."

The Chief motioned towards one of the chairs in front of his desk.

Frank spoke first. "Thanks for seeing me on such short notice."

"Glad you called. Just getting ready to make some rounds. Nothing that can't wait."

"How've you been, Mac?"

"Fine, Frank.?" Chief MacLoone leaned back, the low thud of chair-back meeting wall. He had vowed to do anything for the man now sitting in his office, as long it was legal. Could the debt ever be paid? He didn't know. Did he care? He wasn't sure about that either. "And you?"

Tall, well-built without the protruding belly common to middle-aged men, Frank DeCani's demeanor and dress were those of a gentleman's.

Still Mac's instincts warned of what – danger? Uncertainty threw him off-balance and he didn't much care for the feeling.

"Not bad. Anything new on what happened to Charlie's body?"

"Nothing concrete. Whoever did it had to be able to stay under water for a time. There's amateur scuba divers around here but can't pin it on any of them - yet. As to where they hid the body, that's anyone's guess."

"There's something else."

"What's that?"

"Nell Whitaker. She says she saw Charlie, riding a motorcycle."

The Chief snickered. "Sure she did."

"You know Nell better than I do but she doesn't strike me as, shall we say, unreliable?"

"No, Nell's always been sensible. Why does she think it was Charlie?"

"The hair. Copper color, curly."

"Have to admit. He's the only one I ever knew around here like that." He rubbed his chin. "She tell anyone else?"

"Just Norma. She tries to show that she doesn't believe it. And what about the fires I've heard about?"

"Probably kids. Don't have much to go on there. It's happened before. Just not so often. Usually whoever it is starts bragging and we get them."

Cautiously Frank asked, "Want some help?"

With measured words, Mac answered, "No, but thanks for asking."

"Got any coffee around here?"

"Sure."

Before the Chief reached for the phone, the young woman at the front desk brought in two mugs. Smiling, she handed one to Frank and the other to the Chief. "Here you go, Dad. Mr. DeCani."

"Thanks, hon."

As the door closed behind her, Frank said, "Your daughter is an exceptionally pretty young woman."

"She's a good girl. Like her mother. Always knows what I want before I do. Sometimes I think she bugged my office." Mac cradled the cup in his hands. "Anything else?"

Despite his relaxed pose, Frank caught the hint. "Any recommendations for a motel?"

"Ask my daughter. She'll know." Getting to his feet, Mac held out his hand.

Frank did the same, gave his most friendly smile. "Thanks for your time. "I'll get out of your way now. "

The Chief grinned as they shook hands. "Glad to help. Don't worry. We'll keep you informed."

"Thanks.

Frank stopped at the Chief's daughter's desk. "Excuse me. Your dad says you can lead me to a good motel."

The young woman smiled. "Glad to, Mr. DeCani. There's a bed and breakfast called 'AzLee's B&B'." She shuffled under papers on her desk and came up with a business card. "Here it is."

"AzLee's? Strange name." Frank noted the pink and white flowers around the card's edge.

She laughed. "Kind of. Violet White is the owner. Named the place after her sister – she died a long time ago. Spelled her name like the flower but pronounced Az-lee. Ms Violet says their folks didn't have much schooling and probably didn't know they weren't pronouncing it right." She gave a quick history of Ms. Violet's place.

Outside Frank couldn't miss the officer watching him from across the street, a big, burly guy, arms folded across his chest. *Bet every cop in the county has my license plate. At least I don't have to worry about car thieves.* He nodded at the officer who politely returned it.

Following directions he'd been given, Frank drove through the business section of Olney.

A giant banner stretched across the two lane street; boldly announcing 100th YEAR WHITE SQUIRREL CELEBRATION."

Deep in his own thoughts he hadn't noticed the posters of white squirrels in store windows, at gas stations, cafes, on light poles.

Pedestrians sporting t-shirts emblazed with white squirrels crossed at the stop light. A young man stepped off the curb, approached Frank's open window.

"Hey, Mr. DeCani. Got yours?" He held out caps of various colors, each one with a white squirrel on its bill.

His dour mood lifting, Frank took a green cap and a blue one, handing the young man a hundred dollar bill. "Keep the change."

"Yes, sir!"

Frank chuckled as the money was stuffed in the seller's pocket, not the bag meant for it. The traffic light changed and waving at the future entrepreneur he started down the street, suddenly making a sharp right turn. He continued turning until he was back at the same corner and the young man still hawking.

"Hey, over here!" Frank yelled out his open window.

"Move it!" the kid yelled at a man offering a ten dollar bill, running over to Frank. "You want another cap?"

"How about a program?"

"See Jake. Next corner. He's got 'em."

"Thanks. What's your name?"

"O".

"O?"

The young man blushed. "It's Otho but some folks call me 'O'. Kinda kinky, don't you think?"

"Very kinky." Frank did a thumps up. "Thanks, O."

CHAPTER TWELVE

With program in hand and following directions from the Chief's daughter, Frank soon drove off the state highway at a sign announcing AzLee's B&B. A gigantic gold bow with matching streamers partially hid an arrow pointing to the left, the concrete strip swallowed by thick forest.

He followed the now-graveled road as it descended through trees growing denser with each turn of the tires.

Rounding a curve in the road, the sound of splashing water welcomed him to a bridge of warped wooden planks. He drove slowly across listening and watching the Little Wabash flow over and around the river rocks in its path. The time-worn structure groaned and moaned at the sudden weight of man and vehicle.

Feeling the tires hit solid earth, he took a deep breath, enjoying the unusually warm autumn air reaching far into his lungs.

A new sound erupted from the thick band of timber skirting the river's edge.

Two black horses decorated with garlands of gold ribbons headed a carriage driven by a man dressed in the fashion of a royal coachman from days of old.

Behind him sat an elderly couple, the gentleman's arm draped around the shoulders of the woman beside him. They smiled and waved as they passed. Frank returned the smile, waved, and followed them to AzLee's B&B.

The Chief's daughter had told him a wealthy businessman from Chicago bought the house in 1902 as his retreat, his retirement home. He and his wife continued to live there after their three children left to marry and raise their own families.

When the couple drowned in a boating accident on the Mississippi River the children sold the house. The next owner turned it into a boarding house.

After changing hands several times it was eventually abandoned and stood empty for years until Ms. Violet White bought and resurrected it.

Parking on the side of the road Frank watched as the carriage stopped in front of a two-story grey clap-board house with white shutters.

Party-clad people filled the vast lawn, milling among white linen-topped tables and white lawn chairs, all festooned with gold bows and flowers.

Pots of bright green ferns lined concrete steps leading up to the massive porch where the older folks sat in cushioned chairs, watching over children playing nearby.

Frank made his way through the crowd and stepped inside the open front door.

He stood off to the side of the narrow entryway as a throng of people constantly moved in and out. Rooms to the left and right of the long hallway showed turn-of-the-century elegance.

Crystal chandeliers, red velvet couches, Queen Anne chairs, fireplaces, Persian rugs, highly-polished tables and sideboards. Frank DeCani appreciated the finer things of life and the house reeked with them. He promised himself to ask for a tour.

A voice directing people towards the parlor caught his attention.

He edged towards it and found a small woman in a long Victorian style dress. "Ms. White?"

Limpid blue eyes fixed on him. "Yes?"

"I'm sorry to bother you. My name is Frank DeCani. Chief MacLoone's daughter suggested I see you about a room. If this is a bad time, I can come back tomorrow."

White curls ringed her face, constantly threatening her view. A thin finger captured one and pushed it back. "Oh, yes. I've heard about you. Of course I'll be glad to have you stay here. We're hosting a fiftieth wedding anniversary so it's crazy right now."

She pulled him out of the path of two youngsters burrowing their way towards the door. "Dinner is in about an hour. Why don't you join us for the buffet and afterwards I'll show you the rooms."

Frank's thoughts flew back to Norma waiting for him at Nell's farm. "May I bring a guest?"

Twinkling eyes met his as Ms. Violet asked, "Norma Sue?"

He hung his head. "I keep forgetting there are no secrets in small town America."

"That's right, young man." She patted his arm. "Yes, please bring her." Adding in a more serious tone, "Just no hanky-panky in my rooms. Got it?"

"Yes, ma'am."

"I'll introduce you to the guests of honor later. They'll love having you at their party."

Full of pride at landing such an illustrious guest she moved off to greet new arrivals.

Frank called Norma from his cell phone and told her about Ms. White's invitation.

She told him Nell was spending the night with the sick neighbor again and she'd glad to get out for the evening. He said he'd be right there.

+ + + + +

Thoughts of romance swiftly faded at the sight of Norma waiting by the gate, a frown clouding her face.

Frank stopped the car, got out and reached for her. "What's wrong?"

"There's been another fire. At the Spring Grounds."

He draped an arm around her shoulders. "Tell me."

"The gazebo. It was the only one left, Frank."

"Re-build it."

Leaving the car in the drive, they walked towards the house, Norma's voice betraying the defeat she felt. "It's been fire after fire, Frank. People are saying it's a bad omen. Like what happened before."

"Everyone in town is ready to give up. We'll never raise enough money to rebuild. It's hopeless."

"Not everyone is giving up." He'd been so eager to be with Norma again he'd completely forgotten about his best friend. "When will Bard get here?"

"Any day, I guess. Had some business to take care of in Vegas." Her mood brightened. "He and Nell have some great plans for turning this place into a B&B."

"Have they picked a name for it?" Frank remembered his last night at the farm, seeing Bard and Nell kissing under the willow tree.

"Not yet." Norma squeezed his hand.

Frank took her by the shoulders and stared into the green eyes with flecks of gold he dreamed of every day, every night. "We'll find a way to get your town back like it was. I promise." He turned her around and gave her shoulders a gentle push. Now run upstairs and get ready for a party."

Norma had escaped from Charlie leaving Phoenix with only essentials. While staying with Nell she didn't need evening gowns or cocktail dresses so with no time to shop was forced to borrow a dress from Nell.

Nell's closet held mostly clothes meant for farm work. There were a few outfits for the times she and her husband would drive to St. Louis or Chicago for a concert featuring a favorite virtuoso. They both had enjoyed classical music and spent many evenings with her playing the piano while he accompanied her on his violin.

Norma chose a mauve skirt which on Nell was street length; on Norma it went to the floor. Tying a wide belt around her small waist and folding the top of the skirt over it raised the skirt to her ankles. The matching dove-tailed top meant to be worn outside the skirt became a tunic. A little large but there was no other choice. Nell's shoes were out of the question, at least two sizes too big. Straw-colored sandals from Arizona had to serve.

+ + + + +

They arrived at the B&B just as guests were being ushered into the main dining room for the buffet. Violet White introduced them to the anniversary couple who told her he was the nice man who waved at them on the road.

Norma noticed women openly staring yet Frank seemed comfortable with the attention and while graciously accepting it, gave more time to the men of the town. Smart move, she thought, giving his arm a squeeze.

While asked by other guests to join them, Frank felt obliged to accept Ms. White's invitation to sit at her table.

The buffet bulged with the finest Olney Catering had to offer. When everyone had filled their plates and regained their seats, a toast was offered for the anniversary couple.

Their son gave a short speech as did one of the grandchildren while two of the great-grandchildren added their loud gurgles.

Ms. White had just sat down next to Frank when Chief MacLoone appeared at a table near the door.

She leaned over to Frank, whispered, "He likes to be near an exit, for a quick get-away."

Frank glanced at the Chief looking in their direction.

"He's not here to watch you. It's me he's interested in."

Frank's thick eyebrows went up.

She smiled. "I'll tell you all about it someday if you'd like."

He nodded, smiling slyly at her. "Is that why his wife isn't with him?"

"Oh, no. His wife died about a year ago. Brain tumor. She went fast. Poor man."

Frank wondered at the lack of sympathy in her voice. "I didn't know, Ms. White. I'm sorry."

"Just call me Ms. Violet. Everybody does."

Noticing guests pushing their emptied plates aside, she stood up, taping her champagne glass. "Everyone, an orchestra of Olney's best awaits outside for your dancing pleasure."

The Anniversary Waltz drifted through the windows. Holding hands, the celebrated couple led their guests outside, stepped onto the wooden floor covering a good portion of the front lawn and took the first dance.

Frank waited impatiently for others to join them before leading Norma onto the floor.

All her misgivings disappeared at the look in Frank's eyes when he saw her. That look was still there as he took her in his arms. Her body melded with his and as though one they moved to the music, the skirt floating gracefully around her ankles.

Frank made a mental note to take her shopping in Chicago on Michigan Avenue and to buy her expensive gowns with matching evening coats for cool evenings and furs for the cold nights of winter. He held her l ightly, guiding her through the crowd, his hand gently pressing against the small of her back.

The evening ended early and while the musicians packed up and the cleaning crew arrived, Ms. White scrutinized the guests lingering outside. Confident those staying for the night were still enjoying each other's company, she proudly showed Frank and Norma around the house.

Though all the rooms were taken by out-of-town guests for that evening, she assured Frank one be available the next night.

Frank glanced at Norma, said he'd be back tomorrow.

CHAPTER THIRTEEN

The next day when everyone had left, Ms. Violet White scrutinized her favorite room. A member of the DeCani family in her B&B was already raising eyebrows. And, if she was any judge of people, Norma Sue would be paying him many visits. Sex always made for spicy gossip. What she didn't hear or see she'd concoct.

The house had been built with one bedroom downstairs presumably for a maid or perhaps a secretary as there was a small room next to it which might have been an office.

Four bedrooms were upstairs, including a huge master bedroom she had split into two suites so as to accommodate more guests. These two rooms were her favorites, each flooded with light, facing the back yard, large shade trees shielding the flagstone path to a white octagon gazebo. What a coup it would be if Frank and Norma married at AzLee's B&B and, better yet, stayed for their wedding night.

Town gossips had it that Nell Whitaker was going into business, turning her farm into a B&B with Bard Bolden Doyle's help. Some believed there was more going on between those two than just business.

Ms. Violet's thoughts were of a double wedding. Now wouldn't that be something for the town, the county to talk about?

Moving from one room to the other, Ms. Violet smiled at the beds. Always frugal with her earnings as the best seamstress in the county, they were her one extravagance.

She'd searched through books, magazines, looking for opulence, romance. Finding bed frames similar to those she'd decided on took considerable scouring through yard sales, estate sales.

With materials ordered from the designer houses of St. Louis and Chicago, she copied the experts, designing one room in a masculine tone for businessmen traveling alone.

The other room she'd designated as the honeymoon suite with a king-size brass four-poster bed. She was particularly proud of its umbrella-style canopy of white organdy with a crown at its peak.

Guests were welcomed with fresh flowers in antique vases, a basket of fruit on a mahogany side table flanked by two crystal wine glasses and a bottle of the best wine from Arley's Liquor Barn.

If Frank DeCani was happy at her place, perhaps Norma would want to stay there, too. She might even be convinced to have their wedding at AzLee's B&B. Now wouldn't that be a grand plum in her cap.

A car pulling into the driveway interrupted the daydream. She peered through the sheer curtains to see Frank and Norma arriving. With one last approving look at her handiwork, she hurried downstairs.

Frank asked Norma to check out the room Ms. Violet had selected. If she liked it, fine with him.

While waiting he strolled down the hallway. A broad doorway led to a room holding a baby grand piano. Above it a large portrait covered most of the wall.

Twin girls, perhaps five or six years old, sitting on a piano bench, smiled out from the painting. Frank guessed the piano in the background was the same one now in the room.

The girls wore short white dresses of pink lace and puffy sleeves. Each had a pink bow holding back long blond hair. Two very happy little girls.

He heard Ms. Violet and Norma behind him. "You are so identical. I couldn't even begin to guess which is you."

"Truth is I don't know." Ms. Violet snapped. "Mama never told us. Said it didn't matter. One just like the other." Catching the exchange of looks between her guests, she quickly added in a softer tone, "I'm sorry. I didn't mean that the way it sounded. My sister has been gone a long time and I still miss her."

Norma shook off the persistent uneasiness and squeezed Frank's arm. "The room is lovely. Simply lovely."

"Then it's settled. I'll take it for a month, if that's okay with you, Ms. Violet."

"You can have it for as long as you want. Let me get my reservation book. I'll be right back."

When she had left the room, Frank whispered, "What was that all about?"

"Sounds like Mama was not a nice person."

"I think I'll start looking for a more permanent place. Maybe a small house. Ms. Violet doesn't allow sleep-overs."

"She will if I take a room, too. There's one next to yours with a connecting door." Norma avoided telling him it was the bridal suite.

"Sounds perfect to me."

As their lips touched, Ms. Violet returned. "Here we are. Will you be paying in cash or credit card?"

"Norma likes the room next to mine. She's decided to stay, too. A check okay?"

Hiding her delight, Ms. Violet answered, "Of course, Mr. DeCani. A check will be fine."

"Please, call me Frank."

While he wrote out the check, she whispered to Norma, "You make a lovely couple."

Frank handed over the check, told her they'd be back later.

She said breakfast was at seven, but she was always up by five o'clock if they wanted something earlier. Cocktails were served at six o'clock, dinner at seven.

And please let her know if they wouldn't be in for dinner. She wasn't expecting any other guests for several weeks.

Backing out of the driveway, Frank said, "Think I'll buy a car, something more suitable to this country living. And, also, "he winked, "we'll have it for the long drive back to Phoenix. I'll have you all to myself."

Norma didn't want to think about leaving. "I suppose you'll be paying cash?"

"Think they'll take a check?"

"Who would dare turn down a DeCani?"

"My dad was right. With a good reputation and a good credit rating you can have anything you want. How about lunch before we go shopping?"

CHAPTER FOURTEEN

The Early Bird Café's broad front window displayed several hand-painted versions of white squirrels done by local children.

Inside were white laminated tables atop black pedestals, each with four chrome chairs covered with well-worn red vinyl.

Loud laughter hit Frank and Norma as they entered, apparently coming from a group of senior citizens at a corner table.

Frank and Norma took a table farthest from the noisy group. As she sat down he took the chair directly opposite. "Better to see you, my dear." He grinned slyly.

With coffee pot and two clanking cups in hand, a waitress greeted them with "Mornin', Mr. DeCani, Norma Sue."

"Good morning,." Norma cringed at Betty's high-pitched, little-girl voice, waiting while coffee was poured. "How are you?"

"I'm fine." Betty patted Norma's shoulder. "Hope I didn't upset you telling about Charlie."

She turned to Frank. "Just thought she needed to be ready for the town gossip."

"Haven't heard a thing." Norma nonchalantly sipped the coffee.

"Oh, dear," muttered Betty, asking "What can I get for you folks?"

Norma put the cup down. "Okay, let's have it. What is the latest gossip?"

"I best sit down."

Norma slid over but not until she shot an apologizing look towards Frank.

Betty leaned over the table. "Word is Charlie is back, or at least his ghost is."

Norma laughed. "And he's riding a motorcycle."

The waitress gasped. "You saw him, too?"

"No, Nell did. At least she thought she did."

"Well, if Nell says so, I gotta believe her." A quick look towards the group still chattering away in a far corner gave Betty more time to stay off her feet. "I'm really sorry, Norma Sue."

Despite the glint in the waitress's eyes Norma assured her, "Probably just kids messing around. Charlie's dead. That's all I care about."

Betty smiled. "I'm so glad. You've certainly been through enough hell." She turned to Frank. "You ready for some lunch, Mr. DeCani?"

Frank shrugged, "Wish everyone would just call me Frank."

"Mr. – oops. Excuse me, Frank. Consider it done. This here is the best place to tell somethin' you want spread around. Leave it to me."

"Thank you. I'll remember that." He gave her his best smile. "May we see a menu?"

"Oh, sure thing, Frank. Be right back."

Norma pressed her knee against his. "You've made a new friend."

"Only because everyone around here is convinced I'm head of the Chicago Mob." Frank wasn't smiling.

"You're from Chicago and Italian. Don't take it personally. They'll learn what a good guy you are."

"It's getting tiresome."

Most days he tolerated the common opinion people had of Italians but this wasn't one of them.

When they'd ordered, Frank pulled from his pocket the 100th White Squirrel Celebration program, spreading it open on the table. "This looks interesting. Everything from a parade to a chowder cook-off, even a dance."

Norma slid it across the table. "There's square dancing. Ever done that?"

"No, afraid ballroom and swing are more my style."

"Then maybe it's time you learned. Game for it?"

"Is that a dare, my lady? If so, bring it on."

Her fingers trailed down the schedule of events. "Saturday night. Seven-thirty to ten p.m. at the Community Building in the Olney Park. Be ready, pardner."

He chuckled back, "I'm ready - pardner. Anytime, any place."

"You'll have to get something more fittin', mister."

"Hey, lady. I'm not wearing a tie. What more do you want?" He brushed at his open-neck white shirt under the camelhair sports jacket.

"Oh, puhleeze." She smirked. "You can't show up at a hoe-down lookin' like that."

Betty interrupted them with lunch and politely stayed away until they'd finished eating, then returned, offering dessert.

"No, I don't think so." Frank patted his stomach. "No room for it."

"Same here." Norma wished Betty would go busy herself behind the counter. The lunch crowd hadn't arrived and Betty, with time on her hands asked, "How's Nell, Norma Sue?"

"Fine. She's fine."

"Good. And where you staying, Frank?"

"At AzLee's B&B."

"Now that's a beautiful place." Betty nudged Norma. "Then you met Ms. Violet."

"Yes. Lovely lady."

Betty's eyes scanned the room. "You heard about her and her sister, Azalea?"

"Just that her sister died a long time ago."

"Nobody knows for sure what happened. Azalea disappeared. Some folks said she ran away with a man"

The noisy group finished their visit and headed for the door, calling out to the waitress, "Money's on the table. Thanks, Betty."

"See ya' all tomorrow." She answered, then lowered her voice. "Seems in their early twenties, Azalea fell in love with a young man."

Getting no response she forged on, taking in a great gulp of air when finishing a sentence.

"Violet tried to warn her he was no good. One day Azalea just disappeared. Never heard from her again." Another quick breath. "Broke Ms. Violet's heart. That's why she named her place "AzLee's". That was years and years ago but she keeps hoping Azalea will come back."

"Hey, Betty!" a voice came from the door.
"Oops. Gotta go. Hungry customers. See you later." As she stood up she leaned over the table, whispering, "Some folks got their suspicions. Think it's kinda strange, Ms. Azalea disappearing like that."

Norma smiled. "Every town has its little mysteries. Probably nothing to it. Besides, Betty loves gossip."

Pushing his coffee cup aside, Frank counted out money for their meal with a generous tip for Betty. "Plenty of mysteries around here."

When they got to the rental car, Frank asked, "What do you think about getting a Land Rover? Might be fun to drive. We could go for long rides exploring country roads, wandering through the forest."

"You're quite the romantic." she answered. grinning slyly.

"Look at my inspiration."

There were only two car dealers in town and both said they'd have to order a Land Rover.

Frank didn't want to wait. Norma was certain they'd find one in Effingham only thirty miles up Route 45.

There they found a Jeep dealer eager to show his stock of Land Rovers and sealed the deal by offering to return the rental car, saving Frank the trouble

With the keys to the new vehicle in his hands, Frank suggested they head straight back to Nell's but Norma insisted they first find a men's store. In short order Frank found himself toting a pair of Levis, belt with silver buckle, checkered shirt with bandana, no boots.

He absolutely, positively refused to wear boots, arguing that he'd always danced in city shoes and would continue to do so.

Norma gave in, not wanting to spend any more time on his wardrobe. Anxious to show him the Foundation's progress in Sailor Springs, she said, "It's being cleaned up."

"Then Sailor Springs it is," he assured her, taking her hand, putting it to his lips.

She felt the warmth returning to her cheeks. "You cause a lady to blush, kind sir."

"That's not all I cause a lady to do."

"Am I in danger of being seduced?"

"Every chance I get."

CHAPTER FIFTEEN

As they drove along Highway 121 towards Sailor Springs Norma filled Frank in on the progress of the Historical Foundation.

The Tricklebank twins were remodeling their great-grandfather's two-story house into a tearoom. A local radio station agreed to hold a Radiothon to raise money for the Foundation. Tom Crockett applied to the State for several restoration grants. Plans were made to buy up properties in need of repair as the funds came in and Tom did whatever was necessary, from bribery to flattery, to rid the town of the many abandoned vehicles left in back yards and fields. A local newspaper ran a quarterly newsletter for the Foundation.

Yet excitement created with each step forward ebbed with the recent fires. People were skittish, doubting the project would ever get off the ground.

Norma spotted the faded green sign ahead. "Sailor Springs – Pop. 100" Of all the places she'd traveled, doing publicity, research, book signings, this was where her heart belonged.

She barely glanced at the house a quarter-mile east of the intersection, her birthplace and Lori Anne's, too. It always made her sad, made her think of how life could have been if their mother had lived.

No matter how many years passed, she would never forgive her father. Devastated by his wife's death, he'd gone on drinking binges until raising enough courage to kill himself, stealing even more from his daughters.

Frank made a sharp left off of the paved highway onto the gravel road leading into town.

At the first corner Norma pointed. "Grandma's house."

The car slid to a stop along the side of the road. He remembered his previous visit and their first kiss on Grandma's quilt with the double wedding ring pattern.

Norma, gazing out the open window, said, "It will probably fall down one of these days." Her eyes blurred. "I'm glad Aunt May hasn't been able to find a buyer for it."

Two trees lining the front walk threatened to overtake cracked concrete slabs leading to the house covered with weather-beaten siding. Frank touched her shoulder.

"You love it, don't you?"

"Yes."

"Does your aunt live here?"

"No, she's in San Francisco. She came for the funeral. She'll never come back again."

"Who is handling it for her?"

"A real estate agent in Olney." Dabbing at her tears, Norma squared her shoulders. "Let's go by the tearoom. See how it is coming along."

"Point the way, my lady."

The town was quiet except for barking dogs tied in back yards. Frank frowned at the image in the rear view mirror as dust rose up behind his highly polished new vehicle, telling himself to get used to it.

An elderly man raking leaves in his front lawn yelled, "Hey, Norma Sue!"

"Hey, Gabby !"

Frank slowed the car but Norma warned, "Don't stop. He'll keep us here all day."

He gave the accelerator a push and they moved onto the pavement of Main Street.

Norma pointed out it was once a State Highway, replaced a few years ago by a new road around the town, now used only by the local citizens.

As the car crept along, she continued the history lesson. The white aluminum storage shed served as the U.S. Post Office, boarded-up buildings that years ago housed the barber shop, open one day a month, and the snack shop where used comic books could be had, two for a nickel.

Beside the post office, the only other functional building was the Town Hall where the annual gathering of the town's residents met.

To the north side of the Hall was a block-long empty lot. A few bricks still lay on the ground, evidence of the once two-story bank building whose south wall was used as a movie screen in the summer.

Most everyone in town gathered on Saturday night to watch the movie, usually a western. Blankets were spread out, the smell of fried chicken and home-baked cookies filled the air while adults enjoyed the movie and kids were free to roam the town.

Now it held only weeds, mowed down for the annual town reunion.

On the west side of the street was the Spring Grounds, a fenced field of more weeds.

"It's hard to believe how famous the place was, once upon a time." Norma's mind brought forth memories of playing among the trees, roaming through the first floor of the two-story Billiard Hall, vacant of live humans. Parents warned their children not to venture upstairs, the staircase could crumble any minute they said. The children knew the real reason. Ghosts were up there. If you were very, very quiet, you could hear them moving about.

At the corner Norma said, "Left here." She pointed up the street. "Doc Tricklebank had his home and office up there."

Frank noted the two-story frame house was the only one on the street not being swallowed by vegetation. He parked along side the dirt road while Norma hurried to the front steps, pointing the "Tricklebank Tea Room" sign hanging overhead.

No one answered her knocking. She tried the door. Locked.

Through the narrow windows lining the porch only bare rooms were visible. "I'll try out back," She called to Frank, then disappeared around the side of the house..

He caught up just as she reached the twins standing in front of a pile of smoldering grey ash.

"Ms. Sadie. Ms. Betsy."

Eyes fixed on the ashes, Ms. Betsy raised a hand, then let it fall to her side.

"What happened?"

"It's gone." Ms. Sadie muttered. "Gone. Everything."

"What's gone?"

Frank put his arm around Norma's shoulder. "What's going on?"

The elderly women stood like statues, arms folded tightly over chests.

"Grandpa's diary, the pictures, clothes, gone." Words tumbled from Ms. Betsey's trembling lips. "We put them in the garage while we cleaned up inside and today were going to start moving things back in so we could set up the tearoom."

Norma broke free from Frank and grabbed the sisters. "I am so sorry. So Sorry."

Frank dialed Sheriff Brawley from his cell phone.

Close by, checking out cattle that had knocked down a fence and wandered onto an angry neighbor's front yard, it was only a matter of minutes before John stood with his arms around the sisters, giving what comfort he could, eyes carefully scanning the area.

Assuring them he'd make every effort to find who had done this horrible thing, he examined the fire's remains and the surrounding area. Frank pulled him aside.

"John, do you think this fire was set by the same person who set the others?'

"Could be. Don't have much to go on. I'll ask around, see if anyone saw anything."

"It's a shame all that history is lost."

"The Doc's records had historical value, I'm sure. I'll call in the State Police Crime Scene Technician and the Fire Marshall. They'll take photos, collect whatever evidence there is. Have to put tape around this whole area until then. Give me a hand?"

"You bet."

With the house and yard encased in a circle of wide yellow Crime Scene tape, the Sheriff drove off.

Frank and Norma said their good-byes, telling the sisters to call if they could help. Frank kissed each lady on the cheek and said if there was anything they needed, anything at all, to just let him know.

Walking back to the car he told Norma, "Let's go see Mac. Maybe he'll know something."

Norma crossed the road. "I want to show you something."

"All right."

He followed her over a bent section of the wire fence as she cautioned him to watch for cow pies hidden in the high weeds.

Frank gritted his teeth, determined to stay close behind her.

Cows continued grazing with only an occasional glance in their direction.

They hadn't gone far when Norma stopped. "Here." She pointed at water bubbling from the ground. "This is one of the springs. There used to be a gazebo built around it with benches inside for visitors to sit and breathe in the fumes from the minerals."

Yanking weeds by the handful, she cleared a wide area around the concrete circle protecting the spring. "Got a match?"

Frank fumbled around in his pockets. "Here's a book I picked up at breakfast."

"Give me your handkerchief."

Frank pulled a neatly folded white handkerchief from his pocket. Norma unfolded it and held it over the bubbles, the cloth tent filling with gas. "Now light a match and hold it near the handkerchief."

Frank did as told. Suddenly the bubbles flashed and "poof!"

They both jumped. Laughing at the startled look on Frank's face, Norma handed him the unscathed handkerchief.

"My uncles did that every time they came to visit and I still jump."

Frank loved the sound of fun in her voice. Laughter came easily to her, one of the things he loved about her.

She headed towards a hill opposite the spring and Frank found himself climbing wooden steps built into the earth, half eaten away by time but still there, offering little help up the steep incline.

At the top, Norma reached into the canvas tote hanging from her shoulder. She pulled out a slim green book. Her fingers went to the Post-It note sticking out and flipped the book open. "This is the hotel in its heyday."

She pointed to a blackened area ahead. "When I was a kid there was still some of it left over there. Someone must have burned it down. What a shame."

Frank took the book and studied the photo of a three-story building with two wings spreading out from the centered front entrance.

The accompanying article stated there were a hundred rooms open around the year, with electricity throughout and numerous electric fans. In the kitchen dishes for "the invalid, the convalescent or the rest-seeker" were prepared.

"Maybe we can rebuild it." He told Norma. "Bard's in the business, you know."

"First we have to get people to want to come to Sailor Springs. So few people know about its history." Norma sounded discouraged causing Frank to quickly add, "Then we'll work on that first."

She grinned up him, giving his arm a squeeze. "We can try. Now let's go see Sunflower Lake."

"Lead the way, my lady."

She led him through thickets of maple trees showing signs of the coming winter months. Frank teased as she skipped through the fallen leaves, kicking shades of yellows and golds and red into the air. "You look like a wood nymph, a lovely wood nymph."

"I loved the Spring Grounds in the fall." She danced in circles, reaching down to throw more leaves over her head. "I felt free - like the wind."

At the south end of the property was the lake, unusually clear and blue, surrounded by rapidly fading sunflowers.

A small wooded islet in the lake's center covered with more of the yellow flowers.

Frank tapped Norma's shoulder and pointed to their right.

There by the shore sat a small boy with his dog, a black Labrador, beside him. Frank felt they'd walked into a Norman Rockwell moment.

The dog turned, watching them. Norma put her finger to her lips.

Quietly they stole away, leaving child and dog to dream their dreams.

CHAPTER SIXTEEN

Chief MacLoone stood up as the couple came through his office door. Norma's mind naturally memorized the surroundings. The office held the usual desk, chairs, filing cabinets, potted plant on the window sill.

The Chief drew her attention, an exceptionally good-looking man with hair a dusty brown, neatly parted on the left, cut in the proper style of a police officer. Friendly eyes matched his manner, his face marred only by a deep crease between the eyebrows was proof of his heavy responsibilities. The set of his broad shoulders, the strong chin, the confident walk, the look in his eyes revealed he was in charge.

"Frank. Norma. It's good to see you."

"Good to see you, too, Mac."

When they were seated Frank wasted no time expressing his concern about the recent fires in Sailor Springs. "Can you tell us anything, any clues, any suspects?"

Chief MacLoone leaned back, hands casually resting on the chair's arms. "No, there just isn't anything to go on. We'll keep investigating, of course. Sometimes we get lucky and the arsonist does some bragging and we hear about it. Otherwise, without a witness or some evidence it doesn't look good."

"Think it's kids messing around?"

"Could be. Until now, the fires have been small. I have to hope we get whoever it is before they move up to bigger targets." Mac tried not to show his frustration. "As for Charlie, or Chuck as we knew him, he's dead. That's a fact. His body is missing. Also fact. Some people around here are superstitious, some even believe in witchcraft. Maybe it's a sick joke."

"You're right, Mac. Absolutely. If I can help in any way, you know all you need to do is ask," Frank stood up. "Now we'll get out of your hair."

The Chief had to ask, "You plan on staying a while?"

"This country life is growing on me." He motioned to Norma. "Thanks for your time, Mac."

"Any time, Frank."

As the door closed behind them, Chief MacLoone reached for the phone.

In the county seat of Louisville, Sheriff Brawley glanced at his Caller I.D. before answering his private line. "Hey, Mac."

"John, you got a minute?"

"Sure. What's up?"

"Frank DeCani was just here, with Norma Sue. He's staying at Ms. Violet's place but sounds like he's here for good."

"There a problem, Mac?"

"No, it's just my caution light comes on when an outsider suddenly moves in."

A low chuckle traveled from the other end of the phone. "You getting prejudiced in your old age, Chief?"

Chief MacLoone ignored the question. "Why would a man like this DeCani want to live here, putting aside his obvious attraction to Norma and no one can fault him for that."

"Mac, there's something between you two. It was obvious every time you were in the same room with him. I've got time right now to listen if you've got time to fill me in."

"It's a personal matter, John."

"Come on, Mac. We've kept each other's secrets since we learned to talk."

As brief as possible Chief MacLoone told the Sheriff of Clay County how the well-known DeCani family of Chicago became involved in his life.

"Frank's great-grandfather was Angelo DeCani, a peacemaker in Chicago between the law-abiding Italians and the criminal faction. Never took any money for his efforts. Just felt it was his duty, to help his countrymen."

"One of the good guys."

"The best. Everyone called him 'The Don', a title of respect before it became connected with the Mafia. Angelo succeeded in stopping any trouble before it got out of hand until the criminal element split into two groups. He feared the bad blood would spill over onto the other Italians and tried to make peace between them.

But peace wasn't what they wanted and one day someone walked into his barbershop and shot him. Killed him."

"And of course everyone in the neighborhood was too scared to say or do anything and the police didn't bother to investigate. "

"You got it. Apparently his funeral turned into quite an event, with every Italian who could showing up. Rumors were that Angelo's widow got an envelope of money from a man who promised no harm would ever again visit her family. The DeCani name has never been directly connected with any of the Mafia though PeeWee DeCani is known to be very powerful in Chicago."

"So what does this have to do with you?"

"Frank DeCani saved my father's life and my parents marriage."

"How?"

"Remember the summer Mom and I went to Europe?"

"Sure."

"Before we left, she asked Dad for a divorce. That was why Dad sent us, for her to think things over. He didn't want the divorce. While we were gone, he went to Chicago to visit a doctor friend, they went out, drank too much, my dad got robbed.

"Frank was taking shortcut home after dropping off his date, found Dad in an alley, beat up pretty bad.."

"And, of course, Frank didn't call the cops."

"Dad told him he was a doctor and could take care of himself if Frank would just get him someplace safe."

"So Frank took him home."

"Right. Frank was living with his aunt, his mother had left years before. Dad stayed there a couple of weeks. The aunt swore the DeCani family would forget he had ever been there. Mom and Dad settled their differences and you know the rest of the story."

"Everyone lived happily ever after."

"Yes. And Dad made me swear if a DeCani ever needed anything, anything at all I would help in any way I could."

"So what's the problem?"

"Maybe nothing. I just get uneasy when anyone from the Mob is in my town."

"I did a background check on Frank DeCani and PeeWee. I know you did, too. Frank came up clean. It's his cousin that's the problem.

"Just a little guy but he's got more power in Chicago than Illinois Electric."

"He could mean trouble."

"He's not here now, is he?"

"No, but I'm always on the lookout for him or anybody like him. I know you are, too."

The two lawmen hung up, each glad to have the other on his side.

CHAPTER SEVENTEEN

The search for Dawn Dupree DeCani continued. Larry's wife wouldn't hear of PeeWee staying in a motel, insisting they had a lovely guest room for him as long as needed.

During the days PeeWee learned from Larry about using the Internet and gained great respect for the man's skill.

At night he made contact with the powers of Vegas, rooted out snitches on the streets of the gambling Mecca, used every source he could conjure up.

Many knew who Dawn Dupree DeCani was. No one knew where she was.

Larry combed the Internet for information about her, finding only the usual movie studio hype.

The Screen Actors Guild showed her maiden name as "Smith", no family, found in a basket on the doorstep of a Chicago church when only a few days old. Publicity photos from her movies were easy to come by.

PeeWee made a contact with one of the most notorious of dirt sheets, promising to give the exclusive story in exchange for the truth, if it could be found, a promise he had no intention of honoring.

Larry sent his wife out to Dawn's home in an exclusive section of Beverly Hills to talk to those who worked for her neighbors. Maria had a way of getting people to tell her things they'd tell no one else. She returned to report Dawn owned a mansion bought after the latest of her six divorces. Though her illustrious movie career had gone down hill, her extravagant life style continued.

It wasn't unusual to her to be seen dressed in black leather, tearing down the street on her motorcycle, black with a gold star on each side. No one knew where she went or when she'd return.

County Court simplified Larry's search for marriage licenses, finding each one from a different part of the country. Larry checked the courts for divorce records, each filed in a different town, all in Nevada. The search for her favorite haunts narrowed.

PeeWee then concentrated on expensive resorts, using contacts given by his Nevada cohorts, distributing her studio photo to bus boys, waiters, desk clerks, hotel beauty shops, gift shops. All pointed to the Hyatt Regency, high in the mountains above Reno.

CHAPTER EIGHTEEN

Frank and Norma made a quick trip back to Nell's for their things and had no more than settled in at AzLee's B&B when his cell phone rang.

PeeWee reported that the search for Dawn was narrowing. Frank kept his end of the conversation brief, revealing nothing to Norma, only that his cousin wanted to say hello.

As soon as they hung up, Nell called. Bard would be there in time for dinner. Come on out and join us.

+ + + + +

After a dinner of Nell's special fried chicken with homemade noodles and biscuits, the men were shooed outside while the women straightened up.

Frank told Bard, "Come on, Rags. They want to get rid of us so they can have some girl talk."

"We've got some talking to do, too, Godfather." Bard gave Nell a quick kiss on the cheek and a gentle push towards the kitchen.

Frank took the half-full bottle of wine and two glasses from the buffet table.

When they were settled on the porch steps, filled glasses in hand, Frank got right to the point. "You and Nell are getting married?

"Yes, though she doesn't know it yet."

"Kind of sudden, isn't it?"

Bard chuckled. "Not at all, my friend. Not at all."

Frank watched as his friend's face revealed more than his words. He was obviously in love.

"Everyone in a small town knows everyone else so Nell and I knew each other almost since birth. Went to school with her. Whenever allowed to come to town I wanted only to see her. Course I never said anything to her, didn't feel she'd want anything to do with someone like me, dirt poor, father the town drunk. When Daddy threw me out of the house – I was fourteen years old – I didn't come back until I graduated from high school and then only for my brother.

"I'd promised to get him away from Daddy. Which I did. But I couldn't leave without seeing her."

"There's a quote I read once, forget who said it." His voice softened. "You will have a beautiful life because I have wished it for you."

Swirling the wine, he said, "I've repeated it every day since, hoping to manifest it for her."

"Tell her that."

"I will, when we are alone." Bard put the glass aside, leaned back, elbows on the step behind him. "When I came back I found her working in Olney at the library.

"She was more beautiful than I remembered. She saw me and we spoke only briefly. I've kicked myself ever since. Biggest regret of my life. When I've seen her at the town's reunions, I didn't dare tell her about my feelings because by then I had a wife. Then all the business with Norma and Charlie came along and here I was with Nell, now a widow. No way I was not telling her how I felt."

"And your marriage?"

"Over a long time ago. Big mistake on my part. She got a good settlement out of me. Guess that's all she ever wanted."

"You sure Nell is okay with all this? I mean it is happening pretty fast."

"I asked if I could court her. When the time is right, I'll ask her to marry me."

"And your business in Nevada?"

"All taken care of. I've got a great manager and I can keep track of things from here via computer."

The night's full moon lit the yard, revealing a kitten stalking its prey. Nearby sat an adult cat, perhaps the kitten's mother checking out her offspring's technique.

Bard nudged Frank. Silently they watched as two more kittens joined in the hunt. Low to the ground, tiny tails twitching, they all pounced at something unseen to the humans.

Frank admired their natural way of knowing what to do and how. "Don't know why but that makes me think of the bachelor party in college.

"We didn't make it in time to get arrested."

"If we hadn't been late, we would have been expelled with the others."

"Especially since you were class president." Despite his success in real estate and construction. Bard always felt one step behind Frank.

Frank huffed. "We're were lucky, Rags."

"Yes, we were, Godfather. Your noble efforts to live down the reputation that all Italians are in the Mob would have been for nought."

"And you might have never gotten past your fear of becoming like your drunken father."

"High five, my friend." Bard's hand went up.

Frank's hand met it. "We did good."

"Have you men solved the problems of the world?" Norma called out as she and Nell joined them.

"Yes," Frank stood up, guiding her to the cushioned glider. "All is well tonight."

The phone ringing from the parlor sent Nell back into the house. In a moment she called out "Frank, it's the Chief, for you."

"Stay," he told Norma.

"Yes, master."

"Good girl." His hand raised to pat her head but sparks in her eyes changed his mind.

Frank's talk with Mac changed his playful mood.

"What's wrong?" Bard asked as Frank returned to the porch.

"Charlie's been spotted again."

CHAPTER NINETEEN

The drive to the B&B was as quiet as the night air, only an occasional dog's howling disturbing the silent countryside.

Norma sat staring out the window.

Frank gently drew her to him, his arm around her shoulder. She nuzzled his neck, lips pressing into it's warmth.

Frank could only try to imagine how she felt. What he didn't know was the dream, the recurring nightmare Norma couldn't bring herself to share.

Ms. Violet was in the living room watching television when they arrived. She turned as they came in. Frank waved, index finger to his lips. She merely waved and the couple went upstairs.

Still silent, Frank unlocked the door to Norma's room, stepping aside as she crossed the threshold.

As he reached for the doorknob, she turned, eyes pleading.

He closed the door behind him, folded the bedspread neatly at the end of the bed, took her down into safety and love.

$+ + + + +$

As dawn broke through their bedroom window, Frank woke to see their positions reversed, Norma now entwined around him. Still fully clothed he felt her body trembling, not knowing if she was awake or dreaming. Moist lips brushed against his neck.

He turned over, expecting a kiss, facing instead frightened eyes and tears. He held her tight against him.

She stammered, "Nightmare."

"I'm here. It's all right."

She didn't answer.

The shaking subsided.

He whispered, "Tell me?"

She shook her head.

He handed her the box of tissues from the night stand, and waited.

She sat up, slowly wiped away the tears. In a low but determined voice she began.

"The phone rings. I pick it up and it's Sheila. She's screaming, 'You whore. You filthy whore.

"My husband won't touch me, won't come near me! Let him go. He's mine. Let him go.'

"It tears me apart. I hold the phone at arm's length but the scream is still there. I'm numb, unable to move. I hear sobbing. It's Sheila pleading, begging. 'Please. Please. Give him back to me. Please.' It's always the same."

Frank reached for her but she pushed his hand away.

"I tell myself it's only a dream. It didn't happen that way. Sheila didn't scream, didn't cry when she called me. She'd found our E-mails, knew of our brief affair. She calmly explained Charlie had a sexual addiction, an illness. He had to seduce women. It had been going on for years.

"Except with me it was different. What the doctor had warned her against happened. He became obsessed."

Anger took over Frank's mind and body. Heavy pounding filled the air. What stupid ass workman was causing such a racket? Didn't he know people were still sleeping? Gradually the sound ebbed and he recognized it, his agonizing heart threatening to leap from his chest.

He reached again for her, ignoring her effort to push him away. He had to hold her, share the pain.

"He tried to convince me he really loved me but I didn't, couldn't believe him. Sheila and I wanted revenge, get even with him for playing us both like fools. I got him into bed which wasn't hard to do. I had a gun, Frank."

"Carol, she was a deputy sheriff in Utah, got it for me. She thought I needed it when I was doing some research, taught me to handle it."

Encouraged by Frank's restraint she continued. "Charlie thought I was going to kill him. I twisted his penis until he screamed. Sheila waited outside. I gave her the room key and gun. I don't know what she did after that. You know the rest."

She hesitated, forcing back painful emotions in buried memories. "Some days it all seems so long ago, as though in another lifetime. I wish Sheila had screamed at me. I certainly deserved it."

Frank's fingertips tenderly traced the outline of her lips. "Hush, love. Hush."

CHAPTER TWENTY

While Norma showered, Frank went downstairs, found Ms. Violet in the kitchen preparing breakfast.

"Good morning, Ms. Violet." Seeing the bowl of eggs in her hands he asked, "I hope you don't mind if we have breakfast in our room this morning."

"Of course not." She returned the bowl to the refrigerator. "Is Norma not feeling well? Poor child. She's been through so much."

Unsure what and how much the woman could be trusted with, he said, "This thing about people seeing Charlie is unnerving."

"I can see how that would be. Lot of foolishness, if you ask me. I wasn't at the pond when all that happened but I know once something or someone goes in, they don't come out. Bad place, Soft Pond."

"Maybe some toast or bagels and coffee? I'll take them up."

"I'll fix a tray." Irked at the change in her routine, Ms. Violet smiled sweetly, took her favorite silver tray, filled it with an assortment of her homemade mini-buns, coffee, orange juice, and a yellow rose. "A cheerful touch of nature." She handed the tray to Frank. "I know you'll take good care of that sweet girl."

"I will, Ms. Violet. Thank you."   Though her words were kind, the change in their tone when she spoke of the pond caused his neck muscles to tighten.

As he took to the stairs, the phone in Norma's room rang. A noise from behind caused him to turn, seeing Ms. Violet watching.

"Just want to make sure you get upstairs with that tray."

"I'm fine, Ms. Violet. Thank you."

"You be here for dinner tonight?"

He continued up the stairs, calling back over his shoulder, "We'll let you know."

She didn't answer but he felt her displeasure. To hell with her. Nosey busybody. *Intrigante.*

Sorry for his mean thoughts he promised to do something nice for her.

The call came from Nell. Norma's sister, Lori Anne, and her husband, Ben had left their farm early that morning and were waiting for them at the house. On the drive out Norma voiced her feelings.

"I'm like a human yoyo. One minute my life is great." She moved closer to him. "And the next it's being torn apart."

"I hope I'm included in the 'great' part."

"Of course. I may be naïve about some things but I'm not stupid. You're the best thing that's happened to me since - -."

"Say it. Jack was your husband, Norma, a good man, and a good friend. Don't feel like you're hurting my feelings by mentioning him."

"It's just so damn hard to trust again."

He pulled the car to the side of the road, turning to her. "I love you. You have to know that. And you must believe I'd never, ever hurt you or let anyone hurt you. I want to marry you."

Tears welled in her eyes.

His fingers entwined her auburn curls, bringing her to his lips.

CHAPTER TWENTY-ONE

As they turned off the main road and onto the lane leading to Nell's house, Frank nonchalantly asked, "You mentioned Carol. Who is she?"

"A very good friend. Lives down the block from me. Takes care of things when I'm out of town." She snuggled closer, taking in the masculine scent of his aftershave. "Doesn't hurt to have a Deputy Sheriff as friend."

"Bet she's able to help with research when you're working on a book."

Without losing a beat Norma answered, "Oh, yes. She can find out things about people I can't."

When they reached Nell's house Bard was waiting at the gate. "What's the password?"

"Open the damn gate, Rags."

"The Godfather has arrived." Bard bowing, pulled the gate aside.

Nell, Lori Anne and Ben waited on the porch.

"Hey, everybody!" Norma yelled as Frank parked the car.

Despite the two dogs leaping and barking their own style of welcomes, they managed to reach the porch.

When hugs and handshakes had been shared, Lori Anne poked Ben's arm. "Tell them."

His weather-beaten face cracked with a wide smile. "We're goin' to Europe!"

"Europe?" They yelled in unison.

"More. Tell us more." Norma poked Ben in the other arm.

"Cut that out, you two." He rubbed his arms, moving away from them.

"Let me, Ben." Not waiting for him to answer, she rushed on. "We been talking about it for a long time. Thought we ought to do it before we're too old or sick or something. Went to a travel agent in Effingham. Got a real good deal on - - are you ready for this?"

"Get on with it or -!" Norma put a fist up.

"Okay, okay. We're going around the world!" She waited. They stared at her. "Be gone a whole month." Still nothing. "Somebody say something." She squealed.

Norma cleared her throat. "You never go further than St. Louis or Chicago. Now you're going around the world?"

"Yep." Ben stuck out his chest. "The whole world."

Lori Anne grinned at her husband. "Ben's always had what he thought was a secret yearning to be a photographer."

His hand slipped around her waist. "Can't keep anything from this one."

"With that expensive camera he talked me into letting him buy he's gonna take all the pictures he wants."

"Why now? Any special occasion we ought to be celebrating?" asked Frank.

"Just cause we love each other."

"I'm going to cry." Norma looked for a tissue box. Frank handed her the handkerchief peeking out of his shirt pocket.

Bard gave Nell a knowing glance. "Best reason I know to celebrate."

"This is big news. We ought to do something, go somewhere tonight." Frank said.

"Any idea?" Norma sniffed, eyes still wet with happy tears.

Frank threw a quick glance at his audience. "I am curious about these country opry houses I've been seeing advertised in the local papers."

"You've never been to a country opry, city boy? There's always one going on around here somewhere on the weekends." Ben held up his right hand, two fingers missing. "I played guitar in the bands around here until I lost these. Chain saw."

Lori Anne took the injured hand in hers. "Our kids both play guitar and sing. They're playing over at Mt. Erie tonight, if you'd like to go. I think it's a great way to celebrate."

Norma's eyes sparkled. "It'll be fun, Frank."

"Then let's do it. My treat."

Just outside the small town of Mt. Erie a neon sign flashed, "Country Opry House".

The parking lot was jammed with pickup trucks, vintage cars, and an occasional luxury sedan. Milling around were couples in levis, spangled denim shirts, off-the-shoulder ruffled blouses, checked flannel shirts.

The air was filled with laughter, good fun kidding, and lots of "Howdys" and "How are ya-alls

Ben wore his usual well-worn jeans with denim shirt and black western ribbon tie while Frank compromised with plain tan slacks and white shirt, and a boa tie of turquoise borrowed from Ben. Bard had chosen a simple ensemble of levis with white shirt, rolled sleeves to his elbows, no tie. The women had dressed in snug jeans and denim dovetailed shirts.

Inside the barn-turned-theater on a floor covered with straw, hawkers offered T-shirts and cups advertising the place plus the usual pizza, soft drink, beer, cotton candy, popcorn.

They were directed through a dark passage way to find a room shaped like a half-circle around a stage where musicians were setting up their equipment, tuning instruments. The room was already crowded. Ben pointed to empty seats in the back row.

Towards the front a woman stood on a chair, waving frantically for them to come forward. Nell nudged Norma. "It's a Tricklebank. From New Salem. Must have heard about your boyfriend."

The group made their way down the narrow steps, aware of stares from the crowd.

Norma whispered to Frank, "You're certainly getting a lot of attention."

He merely shrugged, following her down the aisle.

The woman inviting them to join her conducted a scene of musical chairs, moving people out of the needed seats.

"Come on, folks. Put it down." She shoved a beefy hand at Frank. "Glad to meet ya, Frank." She winked. "I heard you didn't like bein' called Mister. You're my kind of guy."

"Thanks." A big woman with arms that looked like they'd spent many hours baling hay and chopping wood, he didn't want her mad at him.

Suddenly the house lights dimmed and a spotlight hit a man standing in the center of the stage.

"Ladies and those you brought with you."

The audience laughed.

"We've got a great show for you, "The Barnstormin' Bad Boys!"

Lights behind him went up, landing on the group of five young men, instruments in hand, dressed in faded jeans and shirts, bandanas of various colors around their necks, long pony tails hanging down their backs, one with a beard to his silver belt buckle.

When the applause and foot stomping died the emcee announced, "We got some new faces out there, folks. Now I'm not gonna point 'em out, might be a mite embarrassin' but you all be extra down-home nice to 'em, you hear?"

"We hear!" the audience screamed.

Frank slouched in his seat while the rows ahead turned to see who was being talked about.

The music began and the show was on.

* * * *

The next morning Norma woke before Frank, his body stretched close against her back.   She studied his sun-kissed hand cupping her breast.

Dark thoughts of Charlie intruded.

Charlie was dead and someone was playing a cruel trick on the whole community.

She hadn't actually seen him sink into the pond as she struggled to get away, crawling through the mud, to Frank.

But the others saw him die.

He had to have died. No one could survive the mud of Soft Pond. Cows had gone into the pond never to surface again. A mere human could not do more.

"Charlie sightings" were reported by sensible, responsible citizens, not crackpots.

Like a horror movie of ghosts and vampires, was he out there? Had he somehow escaped, crawled out, survived?

She remembered the first time she'd escaped his madness.

The morning had started like any other in Arizona, bright summer sun promising another hot day.

Anxious for that first cup of coffee she'd gone downstairs to the kitchen, reached in the cupboard, fingers searching for the box of instant coffee packets, touching something soft.

The box dropped to the counter. A condom, a used condom, fell to the floor, its contents seeping out. Charlie had been in the house - while she'd slept upstairs.

Fearing he was still there she didn't dare go for her purse from the table by the front door. She ran for the car, praying the keys were still hidden underneath. Fighting against rising panic she started the car. A noise on the passenger side, Charlie at the open window, his bright white smile mocking her, dropping her purse on the seat

She'd crashed the car through the garage door, ignored stoplights as she raced towards Frank's restaurant, cowered in the ladies room until hearing, "Norma. Where are you?" Barely able to walk, she'd opened the door, stumbled into Frank's waiting arms.

Now he was in her bed, holding her, loving her. She pushed aside thoughts of Charlie. She wouldn't be afraid again. She kissed the hand holding her gently, lovingly, pressing her closer.

"Happy, Sunshine?"

Slowly she turned, sliding herself against his broad chest, fingers grazing his nipples as she smiled coyly.

"You are a vixen." He whispered, rolling over onto her.

CHAPTER TWENTY-TWO

Ms. Violet greeted them with breakfast on the sun porch after which the couple strolled along the brick walkway through the rose garden now dormant, waiting for on-coming winter.

Casually Frank asked, "How do you feel about staying here at AZLee's?"

"Ms. Violet takes care of everything. I do love being waited on and there's nothing to do except - - ."

"You want to go back to the room?"

"No." She laughed, evading his grasp.

He took his time voicing what had been rankling in his brain. "Would you like to re-build your grand-mother's house?"

"What do you mean?"

"Tear down the old house and rebuild as you remember it, only modernized. I'll give your aunt a fair price and Bard knows the construction business. He'll get me a good deal."

Nora stopped, cocking her head to one side. "You'd do that?"

"On one condition."

"And what might that be?"

He dropped to one knee. "Will you marry me?"

His rehearsed speech seemed lame as her eyes snapped shut, her body stiffened. Getting to his feet, he hurried on.

"I understand how you feel after all the lies you've been told and I've thought long and hard how to prove I love you."

Peering out from under dark lashes she waited

"Norma, you're a brilliant, creative spirit. I can give you all the freedom you need. Whatever else you wish for, I'll give you. All I ask is let me love you, be with you. Forever." From his shirt pocket he took a small black velvet box. "Don't answer me now." He held the box out to her. "Wear this as a reminder of my love. Someday if you wish I'll replace it with a wedding ring."

For a breathless moment Norma gazed at the box, cautiously raised the lid. Tears filled her eyes.

Inside waited an opal cocktail ring, reminiscent of one Jack had given her, a large opal in the center surrounded by smaller opals, bordered by gold lace filigree.

Silently she held out her left hand. Frank slipped the ring on her finger.

Watching from the kitchen window Ms. Violet smiled.

She saw how they looked at each other, touched each other, one always reaching for the other. Frank DeCani's eyes constantly devouring the beautiful Norma looking at him so adoringly. They were lost in each other.

He'd asked her to marry him, gave her a ring. She must have said yes.

Ms. Violet already had her plans. Her gift would be the most lavish wedding anyone in Olney had ever seen. They'd spend their honeymoon at AZLee's B&B. Everything would be perfect. She would see to it.

CHAPTER TWENTY-THREE

One of the few Sailor Springs natives to go to college was Tom Crockett. His family claimed to be direct descendents of the famed Davy Crockett from Tennessee who died at the Alamo in Texas. The single picture they had of Davy showed a tall, slim man with dark hair, a long face with narrow chin, straight nose, and kind eyes. The same description applied to Tom.

Like his ancestor, Tom had an adventurous side and anxious to get on with what promised to be a most exciting journey.

His college years were spent with one goal, to rebuild his town. He studied its history, the people who created it, the causes of its demise.

Armed with a degree in historic preservation, he was ready. He got the word out that about a special meeting being held by the Sailor Springs Historical Foundation at the town hall.

When the couple of dozen people showing up were seated and through visiting with each other he stood in front of them.

"Like many of you, I want to see this town grow. And I congratulate the effort that is being made with fundraising breakfasts and lunches, potluck suppers and the like but we need to bring in new money.

"Tourists spend a lot visiting historical places. Take Williamsburg, Virginia, for instance. It almost disappeared until it was restored. Millions of tourists visit it every year.

"We still have Sailor Springs and our memories. I admit we don't have wealthy philanthropists like Henry Ford and John D. Rockefeller behind us as they did at Williamsburg," he locked eyes with Bard, the wealthiest man to come out of Sailor Springs. "However, I firmly believe if we all work together, our town can be reborn."

Tom went on to explain there were local and national grants available for restoration of historic sites, that it would take time, work, and money.

He asked for volunteers to serve as officers.

Only three raised their hands and unanimously the crowd voted Tom as president, Nell as vice-president, and Norma to serve as both secretary and treasurer until someone agreed to take on one of the offices.

Tom told how delighted he was to see Bard and Frank attending. Both men had connections good for the town and Tom asked Frank to handle publicity.

Frank wanted to know, "Who owns the land?"

"It was abandoned long ago by the owners. I don't even remember who owned it last." Tom gave the others a questioning look. "Anybody know?"

"No." Nell offered. "But I'll find out."

With that settled, Bard offered to take on the fund-raising.

Tom passed out copies of a letter from the State of Illinois.

The Governor would soon announce that the State had awarded the Sailor Springs Historical Foundation a $10,000 grant for the restoration of Dr. Tricklebank's home and office.

Being the last grand residential home remaining in the small rural community that once boasted a glorious resort and spring water industry, the site would serve as a visitors and medical history center for the southeast region of Illinois.

The Tricklebank twins were thrilled. Now they could repair the house completely and make plans for their tearoom.

Tom cautioned them careful records would have to be kept accounting for every penny and to keep in mind the purpose of the grant was the town, not for a tearoom. Their sweet faces portrayed pure innocence.

Once tall women, their backs had rounded, their waists thickened. They dressed each day as though expecting important company, earrings always matching the day's attire, full makeup tastefully applied in keeping with their advanced age.

They had grown old in unison, each still looking exactly like the other. Their once strawberry blond hair now thin, floated like white mist around their heads.

They weren't the only identical twins in the county.

Violet and Azalea White were the other set, born in the same month and year as the Tricklebank girls.

The families celebrated the birthdays together on a day in-between the two, always a big affair, held at the Spring Grounds and attended by anyone who cared to come.

A local band usually played from the back of a flat bed truck and members of the church choirs would sing a few songs. Each family brought food for their own with enough for everyone else and farmers supplied the crowd with fresh watermelons.

The four girls grew up as good friends, sharing secrets and dreams, roaming over the Spring Grounds, searching for treasures, listening for ghosts in the old hotel.

As it is with twins, each was close to her double, thinking and talking alike, finishing other's sentences, feeling what the other was feeling, good or bad.

But Sadie and Betsey always knew the White twins were different.

Though they were much like Sadie and Betsey they seemed to be closer somehow, sharing something their friends didn't.

The Tricklebank girls talked about that late at night in their beds but never quite got their finger on what was so different about the White twins. Not until Azalea fell in love with a young man.

As the romance grew, Violet's jealously of her twin's new lover became obvious to Sadie and Betsey who discussed it in private.

They watched as Violet grew bolder in trying to force the young man to leave her sister alone. Azalea became pale and thin. One day she went for a walk in the country and never came back, according to Violet.

The young man accused Violet of causing Azalea's disappearance, inferring Violet had killed her. He said it publicly and loudly. No one believed him. Shortly afterwards he left town.

Sadie and Betsey tried to continue their friendship but Violet grew distant until the women finally gave up and seldom saw her again.

As Tom pointed out the requirements of the grant money, Nell caught something in the sisters faces as they looked at each other, a ripple of the skin in their cheeks. She glanced at the others in the room but no one seemed to notice.

Sadie and Betsey knew they would do what they wanted. The Governor and the State be hanged. Papa would have his house and his office back like it had been and a lovely tea room to boot.

Next Tom told them of a grant available through the Illinois State Dept. of Commerce and Community Affairs under the category of public facility grants. The total grant money available was $13.32 million and, if they approved, he would work hard to get as much of those funds as possible for their town.

"How would we use the money?" Nell asked.

"I think our top priority should be for a new water system connecting us to the Clay City system. We need new lines installed for the sixty-some homes here and we need fire hydrants. We'll have to get up a formal volunteer fire department."

Everyone agreed and Tom said he'd get right on preparing the proposal. His youthful face grew serious. "Now we need to talk about the fires taking place."

He took a sip from the bottled water at his elbow. "I'm reminded of the fires that plagued the resort from the time the first hotel was built."

He proudly told the history he had so diligently memorized.

"The first sanitarium, The East Lynne Sanatorium and Hotel was destroyed by a tornado. Tom Sailor replaced it with a hotel he named The Glen House. It had a hundred and ten rooms. A suspicious fire destroyed it a year later in 1884. Then he and his wife sold most of the land to a St. Louis businessman, C.E. Hilts.

"Hilts built a another, larger hotel named The Woodlawn. It, too, burned to the ground under suspicious circumstances.

"Some people believed a group of gamblers set the fire in retaliation for not being allowed to use the top floor of the hotel for a gambling parlor. That was in 1894. In 1899 Hilts built an even larger hotel of 200 rooms. Named it The Glendale.

"It burned in 1917. Another fire in the town's business district in the 1920s put many of the shopkeepers out of business. Then the Great Depression came along, the final crushing blow. Sailor Springs never recovered."

Nell asked, "You think the recent fires were set to kee p the outsiders from coming here?"

"Yes. Back then there were some who were afraid of what they would do to the town. And today there are those who do not want changes made. Yes, I think all these fires we're having today are arson."

"Any progress being made in finding out who is doing it?"

"Not that I know of."

Frank spoke up. "According to Chief MacLoone there haven't been anymore fires since the one at the Tricklebank's place." He turned, giving the twin sisters a sympathetic glance.

"Doesn't mean there won't be more." A man in faded bib overalls called out.

"No," agreed Frank. "Let's hope there won't be."

"And pray," another man added.

"Keep your eyes and ears open. Just in case." Tom turned to Bard. "Think you can have some ideas for fundraising ready in a couple of weeks?"

Bard grinned. "I can handle that."

"Great. We'll meet again two weeks from tonight. Okay with everyone?"

Everyone agreed and thanked Tom for taking on the job as head of the project.

CHAPTER TWENTY-FOUR

The next morning after a leisurely breakfast, Frank and Norma waited until Ms. Violet cleared the table before settling down on the white wicker settee in the sunroom.

Norma put aside the bluebook on the history of Clay County Ms. Violet had given her, cradled the green book on the history of Sailor Springs in her hands.

Frank watched patiently as she searched for anything to interest tourists.

"Here's something. There were originally sixteen springs on the grounds and more around town. Maybe we should check and see how many are still there."

He made a note. "Go on."

"The property was purchased by Mrs. Thomas Sailor in 1869 when she exchanged property in Urbana, Ohio for the 400 acres. Her husband visited the property and after having the waters tested, was convinced they held valuable minerals.

"They were originally called 'poison springs' because of the noxious smell but the Indians used them for medicinal purposes. The springs held sodium, potassium, calcium magnesium iron, chlorine, sulphuric and carbonic acid, in various proportions in the individual springs. The grounds were opened to the public in 1878."

From growing up in Chicago Frank had developed the ability to shut out everything around him and concentrate fully on the work at hand. He'd loved school and learning, wanting to know as much as his brain could hold.

Every evening he'd hunker down in Aunt Rosie's front bedroom, eager to finish that day's homework so he'd be ready for the next. Nothing, not even the screeching of streetcars outside tearing through the air disturbed him.

But he couldn't ignore Norma. His eyes followed the curve of her throat, down to the lavender peasant blouse, its ruffle framing smooth, cream-white shoulders. Did bed sheets come in lavender, he wondered.

Her gaze met his and smiling she stood up and took his hand. Without a word they went upstairs.

CHAPTER TWENTY-FIVE

Lunchtime came and went. Ms. Violet heard nothing from Frank and Norma. The longer they were upstairs together the more she smiled, her mind planning their wedding and honeymoon.

When they did appear they were out of the house, in Frank's car and heading down the driveway before she could ask about dinner.

Frank spotted Ms. Violet watching as they escaped into the thick band of timber along the river. She seemed friendly enough but he felt something unsettling below the surface. Better not to let her get involved in their lives.

Norma broke into his thoughts. "What's the hurry?"

His foot eased on the gas pedal. "None, I guess," keeping his voice calm. "Have to remember I'm not in the city anymore. Easy does it. Right?"

"Right. You have to learn to relax."

"Are you hungry?"

Norma glanced at her watch. "It's too late for lunch and too early for dinner. Are you starving?."

"I have worked up an appetite."

"Gee, I wonder how you did that." She said softly, her finger tracing the rim of his ear.

"Don't do that. It tickles."

"I found a ticklish spot? Wow. Didn't think you had any."

He brushed her finger aside. "You're dangerous, lady."

"I know." She kissed his cheek, then pulled away. "How about we go to the park, get a hot dog, take in the sights? Later you can take me some place romantic for dinner."

"The only place I know is Vito's. Okay?"

"Dinner in an Italian restaurant with my own Italian? What more could a woman ask for?"

$$+ + + + +$$

"100th WHITE SQUIRREL CELEBRATION"

The gigantic banner above the entrance to the Olney City Park welcomed all vehicles and walk-ins.

With the event only an hour away volunteers rushed about, setting up picnic tables and benches, booths of arts and crafts were readied for customers. Teenagers waved white squirrel flags from the grandstand as they set up chairs for their high school band.

Inside the dome-topped pavilion food vendors double-checked their offerings in anticipation of the city's health inspectors.

Norma pointed to a young man crossing the wide lawn towards them, arms full of boxes

"Bet he'll know where we can get a good hot dog right now."

"That's 'O'." Frank signaled for him to join them.

The young man nodded in acknowledgement.

"You know him?"

"Otho. That's his real name but he prefers 'O'." Frank winked. "Kinky, you know?"

"Of course. Kinky."

"Hey, Mr. DeCani." O tried to pull a hand free for a handshake but failed.

"Hi, O." Frank lifted boxes from the top of the pile threatening to topple over. "This is Norma."

"Nice to meet you, O." She reached for the remaining boxes.

"No need for that, ma'am. I've got them. Nice to meet you, too. You're the author lady, right?"

She laughed, "Author lady. I like that."

"Where's your white squirrel caps, Mr. DeCani?"

"Must have left them in the car. Where are you taking these?"

O pointed towards the pavilion. "Over there. My aunt'll be selling her cookies. Makes the best German wafer cookies ever." He motioned towards the steps up to the building. "I better get these to her. She brought the bulk of them in the truck this morning. I had to wait for the last batches to come out of the over."

Norma, always alert to unusual names, asked, "Otho is a new name to me. What's its origin?"

"German. Means wealthy. Aunt Betty says my mom named me that 'cause she had great hopes for me. Hope I don't disappoint her."

Hearing sadness in his tone, Norma didn't ask more about his mother who apparently was no longer around. "Aunt Betty? Is that Betty from the café?"

"That's her. I'm staying with her now." O took a step up the staircase, boxes sliding. "Norma, could you take a couple of these? Don't think I'll make it."

"Sure." She gingerly lifted the top boxes. "They smell terrific."

"Aunt Betty'll give you some for helping me."

Doors at the top of the stairs were propped open, Betty's stand just inside. Otho called out, "Look who I brought with."

"Hey, Norma. Hey, Frank." Betty brushed cookie crumbs from her apron. "Looks like my boy needed some help."

"Glad to do it."   Frank put his boxes down, placing beside them those that Norma carried. "Smells delicious here."

Otho gave his aunt a knowing stare, nodding towards the trays already filled.

She caught the hint. "We have wafer sticks, lemon and orange, also cream cookies of chocolate and vanilla, wafer rolls, very crispy and buttery, and - - ." she pointed at Otho, "his favorite, Wolf Waffelrollchen."

"You gotta try 'em to believe 'em." The young man boasted.

When no one could make a decision Betty made up a box of assorted cookies and wafers. "Enjoy." She told Frank, handing over the box. "Now what are you two up to?"

"Hungry for a - - ." Frank's head snapped up. "Hold it." He sniffed at the air. "I smell sausages and green peppers."

"Over there." Betty pointed to the far end of the room. "Vito's cooking. He really smells up the place. That's why I always get this spot by the door. Don't want him spoiling the aroma of my cookies!"

"To me it's a smell from heaven." Frank nudged Norma. "Settle for Italian?"

"Italian for lunch, Italian for dinner. Is there no end to my suffering?"

Frank kissed her hand. "Get used to it."

"Will you two lovebirds get out of here? I've got work to do." Betty gave them a shove, adding, "Tell Vito I'll be over later so save some for me."

A green, white, and red Italian flag fluttered high above the counter of thick breads, olives, grated and sliced cheeses, Italian spices, and copies of "Vito's Famous Family Recipes." On one side of the booth hung a log of Parmesan adding a pungent aroma far beyond the space allowed.

Expertly turning sausages on the grill, watching over green peppers frying in a pan, Vito didn't hear the approaching couple.

Over the sound of hot oil popping, Frank called out, "Hey, Vito."

"Hey, Frankie!" He wiped his hands on the already stained apron.

"I see you are still enjoying your own cooking." Frank poked at the man's wide girth as they shook hands.

"Why not? It's the best."

"Hi, Vito." Norma held out her hand.

"A woman like you doesn't shake hands. She kisses." He lifted her up, planting a noisy one on her lips.

"Put her down, you meatball. She's private property."

Norma, smiling, was gently lowered back to the ground.

"The lady didn't mind, Frankie." Vito gave her a crushing hug before returning to the job at hand. "You want a sandwich?"

"If you have any ready."

Vito waved his hand over the room of vendors rushing about. "Somebody gotta feed them."

Frank bypassed the counter, bent over the grill. "Just like home. Give us two."

Vito grabbed a long loaf of bread, expertly cut it in half lengthwise and then down the middle of each. His hands flew from sausages to peppers to sauce simmering in a huge pot.

"Here you go. Enjoy." He said, handing out the sandwiches wrapped in waxed paper and a supply of napkins.

"You serving dinner tonight? I promised Norma a romantic Italian dinner."

"The wife, she's preparing the dinners. She'll take good care of you. Grab a couple drinks from the cooler."

"Thanks, Vito."

Finding an empty bench Frank and Norma ate in silence as they watched people beginning to gather, strolling from booth to booth.

Norma spotted a woman carrying a stuffed white squirrel. "Excuse me. Where did you get the squirrel? It's adorable."

The woman pointed behind her. "There's a woman back there that makes them. She doesn't make many any more, arthritis, you know. Got this one for my grand-daughter."

"Do I have to shoot ducks or pitch rings to win one?" Frank asked.

"Just pay cash." The woman laughed, hurrying off to find new treasures.

Frank quickly devoured his sandwich. As Norma took the last bite of hers a slice of fried green pepper slid out. She caught it in her napkin making Frank laugh as she put her head back and let it fall into her open mouth.

As she wiped sauce from her lips, he gathered their emptied wrappers and soda cans, depositing all in a nearby bin.

"Now, my good man," Norma told him, with a deep sign of satisfaction, "I need a white squirrel."

"Then you shall have one."

Though the celebration had not opened officially the park teemed with families claiming picnic tables, large groups settling under the trees bringing their tables and chairs.

Young men and women walked hand-in-hand, children chased each other, dogs fought over dropped pieces of food, oldsters settled on benches, babies gurgled and cried.

Norma slipped her hand into Frank's. "It's so nice to be home."

CHAPTER TWENTY-SIX

With a plush white squirrel tucked under her arm and taking the tour of arts and crafts, Norma suggested a walk around the man-made lake.

As they took the wide circular sidewalk, she said, "Tell me about your childhood."

"Why?"

"We women like to know those things. Helps us understand our men folk."

"I hear a slight drawl creeping out."

"Happens every time I come back here. This place, these people, they are my home, my family."

"You belong here."

"Stop avoiding the subject. Tell me - what kind of kid were you?"

Without going into details, he told about his father working with Bugsy Siegel in Las Vegas, his mother disappearing, being raised by Aunt Rosie.

"You grew up in Chicago?"

"Yes. With Aunt Rosie, and her family. She was a widow, raised three girls, Little Mary that you've met, the other two are married and live in the suburbs now. And one son, PeeWee."

"The little man with the big gun." Norma shook away memories of the day at Soft Pond, Charlie holding her, a knife at her throat, PeeWee coming out of the woods, gun in hand. "That day your family showed up at Nell's unannounced - I'll never forget Aunt Rosie saying, 'You got a problem, we got a problem.' Now that's family. I like that."

"PeeWee told them the woman I loved was being stalked - they had to get involved."

"I'm certainly glad they did." A group of joggers on the other side of the lake reminded her she hadn't run in a long time. Must get back to the habit of doing that every morning. "Go on."

Frank lead her to a bench facing the lake. "When I was a kid I had rheumatic fever. Doctor prescribed carrots, lots of carrots and bed rest. To this day I'm not fond of carrots."

"Scratch carrots from the list."

"I'd sneak out, get into a baseball game in the school yard. My Uncle Mike, a great guy, he always knew where to find me. He'd grab me by the back of the neck, give me a shaking, drag me home, where Aunt Rosie would give me a few good smacks on the backside, then send me back to bed. Next chance I got, I'd be out again."

"You must have missed a lot of school."

"Yes, had two relapses of the fever but I made it up by skipping two grades in one year."

"Genius?"

He held her closer. "No, just bored being at home. My teacher sent over the lessons and books from the library. I read everything I could get my hands on. There wasn't anything else to do. No TV, no Internet. Just books."

"Big family?"

"Cousins galore. Always someone to play with, fight with. And any day was a reason for a party."

She curled into his warmth. "Go on."

"Sunday was special. Started with early Mass. Then the whole family came over to Aunt Rosie's."

Norma felt him relax as he talked about those days so long ago.

"Sunday breakfast in Aunt Rosie's kitchen was special. It wasn't just the food, which of course was great. It was the fun of everyone being together, joking around, telling stories about the neighbors. Anyone needing a job had only to ask. Somebody'd know someone hiring."

A deep chuckle rose from his throat. "One time cousin Mikey and I double-dated at a neighborhood dance. We got home in the wee hours. He decided to stay over with me at Aunt Rosie's. We didn't bother undressing, just fell into bed in our suits. We couldn't have been asleep but a couple of hours when Aunt Rosie came shaking us, yelling, 'Time for Mass.' Being good Catholic boys, we got up and went to church. She never said anything about us looking like we'd slept in our clothes which, of course, we did."

Norma, engrossed in Frank's story, hadn't noticed the joggers approaching until they were directly in front of the bench. One doffed his cap. Norma gasped, grasping Frank's hand.

"What's wrong?"

"Charlie."

He jumped up. "Where?"

"Joggers."

The group had left the sidewalk, swallowed up by the increasing crowd.

"Are you sure?" Frank sat down, staring at her pale face.

"The hair. The smile. No mistake."

"I'll find Mac. He has to be here."

"Saw the Chief's car over —-." Norma held her stomach, sweat showing on her forehead. "I - I'm going to be sick."

Frank yelled, "Someone get a doctor!"

Picnickers nearby surrounded them.

"What's wrong?"

"What happened?"

A little boy grabbed a woman's leg. "Is she dead?"

"Get the hell outa the way!" a deep voice demanded. The woman from the Country Opry shoved through the crowd. "Got trouble here, Frank?"

Norma stumbled to her feet, still clutching her stomach. She turned, doubling over, falling to the ground, retching.

The woman grabbed her, holding her head, screaming, "Somebody get some water and a towel. The rest of you - scram!"

One of the joggers came running up. "Need some help, Sarah?"

"Norma musta ate too much. Just gettin' rid of it. She'll be fine, Sam."

Frank pulled the jogger aside. "You know those you were running with?"

"Just about. There were some newcomers, probably out-of-town visitors. Why?"

"Notice a guy with red hair?"

"No, afraid not."

"You seen Chief MacLoone?"

"I'll find him."

"If I can ask another favor - - ."

"Sure thing."

"I assume you drive?"

"Everything from a tractor to a hot rod."

"Good. Bring my car over here?" He held out his car keys, told how and where to find it.

"My pleasure, Frank. Be right back."

A young girl handed Sarah a wet towel.

Fighting for air, Norma sat up, grateful for Sarah wiping her still-ashen face. "I'm sorry." She whispered.

"It's okay, honey. You'll be okay now." Sarah looked up at Frank hovering over them. "You best take her home."

"Of course.   Norma, you rest a minute." He'd caught sight of Mac coming across the lawn.

After a few moments the two men parted. Still weak and shaking, Norma said she wanted to leave. Frank started to carry her but the set of her jaw vetoed that idea. Offering his arm, he thanked Sarah and said if they ever needed anything, just give him a call. Ideas of going to the dance were forgotten.

CHAPTER TWENTY-SEVEN

Miss Violet tore the rake through dead leaves and twigs, forming them into large piles around the back yard. *All this talk about Soft Pond. Why can't these fools leave the past alone? It's over, gone. Why did Azalea have to fall in love with a man? Hadn't she been told how evil, how deceitful they were? She knew Daddy cheated on Mother again and again, never bothered to hide his affairs from her or the town people, causing us so much pain and embarrassment we wanted to die. Only women, God-fearing, faithful, loving women understand the need for loyal, faithful lovers. I had no choice but to try to save my sister, my twin, my other self from a life of degradation.*

Bitter-sweet memories flooded back. She had done the unthinkable, encouraging the town's only dentist to call on her. When his advances became arduous she rejected him, dropping hints that she was upset because Azalea preferred women instead of men. That was so wrong, completely against God's rules. She loved her sister but she was evil, taken over by the Devil.

Hungrily eyeing her voluptuous figure, her suitor agreed.

The next evening during a long walk under a full moon Miss Violet didn't resist when his hand rested near a breast.

She led him to believe if he helped her rid her beloved sister of her evil ways - permanently - she would gladly give herself to him.

But how, he asked.

Maybe, she said demurely, though she didn't know much about those things, if he knew of a strong sleeping pill or perhaps a pain killer that would let her simply drift off into a deep sleep never to awaken, something fast acting, no suffering. She certainly didn't want her dear sister to suffer. That would be inhumane.

After giving the idea much consideration as he laid in bed alone, frustrated, he consented.

At Azalea's next teeth cleaning, the passionate dentist told her she needed a special procedure that required a shot of Novocain.

The pain killer would wear off in a few hours but he was giving her a liquid medication to handle pain that would surely follow.

Azalea consented and made the appointment.

On their next date, he was hard put to keep his eyes off Violet's exposed cleavage. Pressing forward, he explained between kisses that the medication would work quickly, he said, with no suffering if Azalea took the prescribed amount.

But too little or too much and she would suffer with convulsions, blurred vision, headache, vomiting. Very unpleasant to watch.

Violet pictured her sister's fatal sleep. Soon, very soon, she smiled and let her lover have his way with her.

Violet, growing more angry every day at Azalea's refusal to continue their intimate sisterly relationship, desiring only her new lover. Azalea didn't understand the suffering she had caused her loving sister. She wanted her to know.

After the dental appointment and knowing timing was crucial, Violet suggested to Azalea that they go on a picnic in the quiet woods near Soft Pond.

When the right time came she reminded Azalea to take her medication. "Let me do that, dear." She poured the prescribed dose.

Azalea obediently took it.

Violet offered another, saying, "That dear dentist said you could take two if you wanted. Might help you heal faster. And I do hate when you don't feel well."

Azalea smiled and swallowed the second dose.

Violet waited. "How are you feeling, my sweet?"

"Fine. In fact, I do feel better. Thank you."

"You're very welcome. Shall we go home now?"

"If you like."

As they gathered the tablecloth spread out on the ground along with any leftovers and placed them in the wicker basket, Violet steamed inside. What did that fool man give her? She's not dead. Why isn't she dead?

They weren't in the house five minutes when Violet said she had a terrible toothache and needed to see the dentist immediately. Azalea assumed she'd go with her and Violet couldn't think of a way to stop her.

While Azalea waited in the reception area of the dentist's office, Violet was inside, fighting to keep her voice down. She demanded he tell his receptionist and assistant not to disturb them.

That done, she attacked in a low, menacing voice. "I gave her two doses. Where is she now? In your office. She's supposed to be dead! Why isn't she dead?"

Prepared for this moment, he took a long, deep breath. "Violet, my love - - ."

"Don't you dare 'my love' me! What happened?"

"I couldn't do it."

Violet's eyes glared, mouth tightened.

He put his hands up, surrendering the truth. "You know I'd do anything for you and I tried, I really did. But murder? No, I couldn't. I'm sorry."

"Sorry? You bastard. I gave myself to you and what did I get in return - betrayal! You bastard! I'll get you for this. I promise you that." She spat in his face.

"I'm sure you will, Violet." He wiped his face, opened the door for her.

As Violet hurried home, she cooled down. He was right. How could she think of such a thing? She would make it up to her sister, bake her a rhubarb pie. Azalea loved rhubarb pie.

+ + + + +

The memories of those days long gone by dissolved at the sound of crunching gravel in the B&B's driveway. Violet hurried to the driveway, saw Frank's car but he and Norma were already in the house and on the stairs to their rooms, managing to sidestep any questions.

As she came in the front door, Frank called down, "We'll be staying in for dinner. Something light, if it's not too much trouble." An Italian dinner would have to wait for another night.

"That's fine, Frank." Miss Violet noticed the box of cookies Frank left on the hall table. "This box, is it yours?"

"Betty sent them over. Homemade. Help yourself." He closed the exchange with, "See you later."

Miss Violet peered into the box. "German, no doubt." She went into the kitchen, leaving the box behind.

Dinner was light as was the conversation with Frank doing most of the talking, skirting any topic close to the incident at the lake, Charlie's missing body, the Sheriff.

Norma smiled, kept her attention on cutting the salad, wiping invisible bits of food from her mouth, straightening her collar; all much too often and unnecessary thought Violet.

After dinner Violet told them she needed to rake the front lawn. Perhaps they would enjoy sitting outside.

Norma leaned towards Frank. "Shall we?"

"Of course."

"Good." Violet began clearing the table. "There's a couple of warm jackets on the coat rack by the front door. Help yourself. It'll be down right chilly when the sun goes down."

"That's very nice. Thank you."

The incense of burning leaves filled the evening air. Red maple and oak trees covered the lawn with their fallen colors.

Violet busied herself with the raking while Frank and Norma watched from the veranda. Frank had offered to help but she said no, she liked doing it. He wondered out loud how long they could stay outside, the air growing cooler as the sun moved lower in the sky.

She laid down the rake. "I know what you need."

Coming up on the stairs she opened a white wicker chest, pulling out a woolen afghan of browns and greens. "Told you it would get chilly."

Frank smiled as she tucked it around the two of them. "Thank you. We'll stay out here as long as we can. I haven't felt air like this in years."

Miss Violet nodded and returned to the yard, setting fire to the great heaps of color, turning them to ash.

Norma was quiet, too quiet. Perhaps talking about Sailor Springs would help take her away from whatever she was thinking.

Attempting to bring her back from wherever her mind was, Frank said, "Tom Crockett seems to know what he's talking about, getting grants to restore Sailor Springs."

"Yes. He's done the research." She loosened the afghan, folding it back to her waist. "But it's going to take a lot of hard work. And money. There aren't any young people offering to help the Foundation either. And they don't have much money."

"It will take some high rollers interested in preserving historical places." Frank offered, smiling as she pushed off the afghan.

She curled her legs underneath her. "But how to find them?"

"Bard already has some ideas, I'm sure. I'll talk to him tomorrow."

"I'd like to stay here and work on Grandma's manuscript. My brain mulled it around and came up with a few ideas."

"You make it sound like it's a separate entity."

"Seems to work better when I get out of its way."

"Excuse me?"

"If I get busy with something else -," she glanced at him, "it works in the background until it has the information I need. Crazy, I know, but we writers have to be a little crazy."

"If you say so."

CHAPTER TWENTY-EIGHT

The next morning started much like the previous except Norma asked for a carafe of coffee in her room. She planned to spend the day working on a new story.

Violet, picturing future headlines in the newspaper, "Local Author Writes Pulitzer Prize Winning Book at AzLee's B&B", said she'd bring it up shortly.

Bard called, said he had an appointment that afternoon with a reporter at the TV station in Effingham, would like Frank to go with him.

Uneasy with leaving Norma with Ms. Violet, though he wasn't sure why that bothered him, Frank insisted on her riding out with him to Nell's and staying there until he and Bard got back.

With the men gone, Nell tackled her chores and Norma tried to concentrate on Grandma's story but her mind kept wandering.

To get back on track she practiced her usual distractions, running in place until breathless, stretching exercises, talking to herself in the mirror, drawing an outline of her hand on a piece of paper. Nothing worked. In desperation she phoned Lori Anne.

"Hi, Sis. Are you busy?"

"No, just figuring out what to take on a world tour, nothing important. What's up with you?"

"I'm sorry. You want to call me later?"

"Come on. You have something on your mind. What is it?"

"I can't get any work done. Frank is off to Effingham with Bard. They're meeting with someone at the TV station so I'm out at Nell's trying to work on this story but my mind won't let me. I think I need to get out of here, do something fun."

"Fun, you want fun."

"Yes. Let's go shopping. We haven't done that in a long time, just you and me. Is there a mall around here?"

"Not like in the big city. But there is a new food store that opened about a month or so ago.

"I haven't been there but hear tell it's the cheapest around. You bag your own groceries. Does that sound like fun?"

"Anything is better than sitting here tearing my hair out. Pick me up?"

"Sure, big sister. I'll be there in about an hour. Have to find Ben and tell him."

"Great. I'll be ready."

Norma found Nell in the barn, invited her to come with them but Nell said she had too much to do and food shopping didn't sound like fun to her.

Lori Anne pulled up to the gate in exactly an hour which didn't surprise Norma.

Her friends thought her obsessed with time, always arriving at appointments on the dot. She'd counter with saying it was a family trait. If she was obsessed, her sister was, too.

They drove into the nearby town of Flora, had lunch at the café, endured Betty's latest collection of town gossip and headed for the new store.

Inside it was more of a warehouse than a grocery store, huge bins of canned goods, cereal boxes, paper products, hardware items, garden supplies, whatever a person wanted. Lori Anne stocked up on necessities for the coming winter as she counted on being snowed in for days at a time until the county cleared the roads.

Getting in one of the long lines at the checkout registers Lori Anne insisted on putting their purchases on the conveyer belt while Norma did the bagging, avoiding their usual fight about who paid.

With a cart-full they hauled it out to the truck and headed back to Lori Anne's farm. Ben wasn't in sight but the sisters got it all in the house and stored away in the pantry and cupboards.

As the last of the canned goods were in the pantry, Lori Anne turned to Norma. "You know this is ridiculous."

Lori Anne's eyes twinkled. Norma knew what was coming. It always happened when they were together. Like little girls, the slightest thing turned them into laughing hyenas.

Cautiously she asked, "Why?"

"Think about it. We go in the store. Take the stuff off the shelf. Put it in the cart. Take it out of the cart. Put it on the counter. Take it off the counter. Put it in a bag. Put the bag in the cart." She leaned against the refrigerator.

"Take the bag out of the cart. Put it in the car. Take it out of the car. Put it on the table. Put it on the shelf. IT"S CRAZY!"

Both women bent over with the contagious laughter that brought, tears streaming from their eyes.

"Stop it!" gasped Norma. "I'm going to wet my pants."

"I - I can't help it!" sputtered Lori Anne. "Quit looking at me!"

"I can't." Norma sputtered back, pulling herself along the kitchen counter, into the powder room. Before coming out she yelled, "Are you finished?"

A tiny voice answered, "I think so."

"I'm not coming out until you promise not to laugh anymore."

"I promise."

Norma opened the door to find Lori Anne standing at the window, shoulders shaking.

That familiar feeling growing again, Norma warned, "Don't you turn around. You're still doing it."

"Okay." her sister answered in that tiny voice.

"Make some coffee. Get your mind off that store."

"But", Lori Anne squeaked, "It is so funny."

Norma laughed. "I know. It is."

"Now I have to go." Lori Anne scooted past Norma, making it safely to the powder room.

Wiping her eyes as she came out, she saw Norma at the sink, running water over her wrists. "What are you doing?"

"Getting myself under control. Cold water on the wrists is a shock, stops me from crying or, in this case, laughing. Try it."

"No thanks. I'm fine now."

"It's been years since I laughed like that." Norma raised her arms and stretched. "Felt good."

"Me too. Guess we just forget how to have fun."

"Well, baby sister. Now that I'm staying we'll do it more often."

"Deal. Good to have you home." Lori Anne's arms opened. The two held each other, memories of happier times flooding their minds.

"Now," Norma said, pulling back. "I'm hungry. How about you?"

"Got some of Betty's lemon wafers and cream cookies, the ones with chocolate. Okay?"

"Sure."

Lori Anne went about making coffee while Norma told her what she'd learned about Grandma's life from the manuscript they'd found at old house.

CHAPTER TWENTY-NINE

In his search for the Sailor Springs arsonist Sheriff Brawley concentrated on the few people living close to the Tricklebank house. Perhaps someone heard or saw something.

Behind the house on a lane running to the edge of the woods was Betty Helmutt's home, a one-hundred year old, two-story place that she spent every dollar possible on restoring.

Since Otho Helmutt had been living with her, he'd acquired the reputation of being a hard worker. A pleasant enough young man with big blue eyes under long thick lashes, he had no trouble worming handyman jobs out of Aunt Betty's friends and neighbors. Problem was he never arrived on time.

That trait did not sit well with Betty and while he was out one day she set his clock 30 minutes fast. Complaints of his chronic lateness stopped which he attributed to his charming ways.

Figuring Otho might have been up early the morning of the fire, the Sheriff tracked him down to his current undertaking, selling caps on Main Street.

What time had he gotten up that day? Alarm went off at five o'clock, left the house about half an hour later. Had a job in Clay City. Hadn't seen or heard anything out of the way.

Had he seen anyone lurking around before that, maybe casing the place? No, not a thing.

Betty, next on the list, said she got up that morning about six-thirty, hadn't even heard Otho leave. Course she'd always been a sound sleeper, never used an alarm. Seem to have her own internal clock. Just tell herself what time to get up and she did.

While the Sheriff talked with others in the area, Chief MacLoone's daughter was convincing him to hire help around the house, inside and out. Neither one of them had the time or even the desire to do all the things Mom had done He needed a part-time gardener and a full-time housekeeper. Finally winning him over she was sent to hire a housekeeper while he went after Otho for the outside job.

"I'd be honored to work for you,
Chief. I can start tomorrow if you like," Otho told him.

"Great. Come on over in the morning and I'll show you where to start on getting the yard up to snuff and then we'll work out a schedule, like maybe twice a month. You have to be there no later than seven o'clock. Okay?"

"You got it, Chief. Seven it is."

"Thanks. See you then."

Mac knew Otho had a reputation for always being late, but folks said lately he got where he was supposed to be on time. Just to make sure, Mac headed for the Early Bird Café.

When told of Otho's new job and asked about being punctual, Betty grinned. "I can guarantee he'll be on time, Chief. I set his clock thirty minutes ahead. Been on time ever since."

"I'm surprised he hasn't caught on."

"You know young people, Mac. They're so wrapped up in themselves they can't see something right under their noses."

Despite Otho's past troubles, Mac liked the young man.

He'd stayed on the straight and narrow in Olney. Yet, what Betty told about the clock gave him pause.

After reviewing the Sheriff's report on the fire at Tricklebanks, he thought, "If Otho set the alarm earlier than usual, half an hour, even an hour, and not realizing Betty had also reset it, and the fire was started between midnight and five o'clock that morning, he could have could have done it."

The theory was full of holes but used right but be just the ticket to get Otho to confess. He called John.

Sheriff John Brawley decided to check the clock himself. Like most everyone in town, Betty never locked her doors.

He let himself in and went upstairs to Otho's room. He wasn't surprised to find it neat and clean. Betty was known for her cleanliness. People said even the springs on her antique bed were spotless.

The clock showed three p.m., his watch displayed one o'clock. The young man forgot to reset it. Otho would do that. He couldn't always be depended on to do what needed to be done.

But why would he set the fires? To make money. Who paid him? Who would want to destroy the things that could help rebuild the town, benefiting everyone? Some people objected to changing things but the Sheriff didn't think anyone would go so far as to destroy property, possibly hurting or even killing someone.

Still, Betty's house did sit on the edge of the woods, was the closest neighbor to Dr. Tricklebank's office. Otho could easily have slipped out without her knowing. In the early morning darkness he wouldn't have been seen.

Sheriff John Brawley knew, as much as he hated the idea, he had a prime suspect.

CHAPTER THIRTY

Conversation was scare on the drive to Effingham, Frank and Bard each deep in their own thoughts. Until Frank's cell phone rang.

Frank listened intently, saying nothing except, "Thanks, Cuz. Good work."

As he hung up, they drove under a bower of trees. A roaring sound came from behind, a motorcycle sped past, disappearing off the pavement into a field.

Frank yelled, "Charlie! Turn around! Go back!"

"Shouldn't we try to catch him?" Bard slowed the car.

"Never do it. I have to get to Norma." Frank repeated, "Turn the damn car around."

Bard did a sharp u-turn and headed back. "What's going on?"

Frank's right foot pressed into the floor boards. "Move it!"

"Any faster and I'll get us killed." Bard kept a tight grip on the steering wheel. "Now tell me."

"Have to call Nell first."

+ + + + +

Norma wasn't at the farm, Nell said. Lori Anne had picked her up and they were going shopping at a new grocery store just outside Flora on Route 51.

"You see what Lori Anne was driving?"

"No, Frank. Sorry. You want me to call Mac?"

Bard pointed down the road. "There."

"We found it. If you hear from her, call me."

Pulling in front of the store, Frank was out and running before the car stopped, yelling, "Check the lot."

Bard drove slowly around the parking lot, scouring for the women. Not spotting them, he parked near the store's entrance, then stood inside, watching the checkout lanes.

Frank appeared between aisles, waving at Bard who answered with a shake of his head. Exasperated, Frank caught a stock boy, ordered him to get the manager. The boy ran off to tell his boss that gangster fella from Chicago wanted him.

The store's speaker system blared out the announcement, grabbing the attention of several customers and a cashier who remembered seeing the sisters. They had a cartful, lots of frozen food, the cashier said. Probably headed home.

Getting directions, Frank and Bard raced out of town, down gravel roads between fences holding back cows and horses, roads unmarked that seemed to go nowhere until the house came into view at the end of a long narrow lane.

Dirt flew as the car skidded to a stop at the porch. The two men leaped up the steps, tore through the front door, Frank yelling, "Norma! Norma!" A furtive glance in the living room, dining room -found no one. "Kitchen! Have to be in the kitchen!"

Hearts sank at the sight of broken chairs, over-turned table, floor littered with shattered glasses, dishes. "Norma, Lori Anne, are you here?"

"Frank!"

"Norma!"

Bard pointed at a closed door. He opened it slowly, flinched at the site of the sisters clinging to each other, cowering against the wall.

"What happened here?" Bard asked, helping them out of the small room. "Are you all right? Where's Ben?"

Voice quivering, Lori Anne answered, "In the - fields."

Bard pulled a chair closer, guided her onto it. "My phone -." She pointed to her purse on the sink. "Couldn't reach it."

Frank clutched Norma tightly, willing away the shaking. "Charlie, Frank. How - ?" Norma stared wide-eyed, begging for an answer.

Frank's face turned hard. "Shhhhhh, Later. Later. Shhhhhhh. "

"He broke through the back door. It happened so fast we barely got a glimpse of him." Regaining control of her voice, Lori Anne saw the destruction. "Oh, my God. Look at what he's done." She broke down in tears.

Norma reached a hand out to her baby sister. "All of a sudden it got quiet; although we heard the motorcycle start up, we were afraid he was still here."

Frank loosened his hold on her, ran his hands down her arms. "You okay?" Then to Lori Anne, "How about you?"

Norma took a deep breath. "We're okay. Just shook up. Right, Sis?"

Lori Anne managed a weak smile. "Right, Sis."

"Good." Frank yanked at the wall phone, then slammed it back. "Lori Anne, Mac says there's a network that notifies everyone of disasters, accidents, the like. How do we do that?"

Still sobbing over her beloved kitchen now in ruins, she mumbled, "Nell. Tell her."

Nell said she'd get right on it and hung up. Frank replaced the dead phone in its cradle.

A loud screech sounded; a flashing light glowed from a black box sitting unnoticed on a shelf of the open pantry.

"CB." Lori Anne got to her feet and wiping at the tears, staggered to the pantry.

Bard saw her about to fall, catching her arm just as she pushed a red button.

Nell's voice filled the room, "Alert! Alert!" In a crisp, commanding voice she gave a brief account of the break-in and vandalism, description of the culprit, and to call the Sheriff's office if spotted. Lori Anne said the same would go out over all phones in the county.

"I'll call the Sheriff, the Chief." Frank took out his cell phone. Lori Anne stopped him, said no need, he'd know already.

"Farmers take care of each other, Frank." Norma added.

"We're all uptight." Bard asked, "You got any booze around here?"

Lori Anne pointed towards the pantry. "Brandy from Christmas."

Not needing to ask, Norma handed her the purse. Lori Anne called Ben and before hanging up the sound of a tractor's roar thundered through the phone.

Coming from the field, Ben's anger grew with each turn of the tractor's wheels. He barreled through the fence, stopping just short of the back door. His great girth filled the doorway.

"I'm fine, honey." Lori Anne shouted, "Honest."

Ben snatched her up into his arms. "Don't you worry, babe. I'll kill the bastard myself."

Frank clamped his lips together. This was not the time to tell Norma about the call from PeeWee, not until they were alone.

Bard salvaged a few unbroken glasses, up-righted the table, and poured generous amounts of the brandy. No one spoke as they sat down, waited silently for the liquor to take hold.

With Norma's hand at his lips, Frank vowed, "I won't leave you alone again."

Lori Anne gazed up at her husband who refused to let go of her.

"And, Ben, don't you go killin' anyone. I'm not missin' out on a trip around the world just because you're in jail. You hear?"

Ben kissed her forehead. "I hear, woman."

Norma slid her emptied glass toward Bard for a refill. "We need to bait him. Like we did before."

"Oh no, you don't". Frank glared. "You're not putting yourself in danger again. Forget about it."

He had not forgotten the panic he felt watching her from Nell's upstairs as she walked across the field, put up her easel, waiting for Charlie to appear, the terror of seeing him sneak up from behind, grabbing her, dragging her to his truck, not going to Soft Pond where PeeWee waited, taking off in the opposite direction.

The Sheriff and the Chief of Police had ordered all roads blocked, the whole county searched.

Woman's intuition warned Charlie might have taken Norma to the cemetery.

A few years before kids had broken into one of the mausoleums, shooting up drugs. Could be Charlie'd figure no one would think of that place.

Nell gave Thunder Norma's sweater to sniff. The dog led them to the mausoleum and evidence Norma had been there, then tracked the couple to the edge of the woods where oil spots were still fresh and tire tracks leading in the direction of the pond. The perfect place for a murder.

Frank wasn't letting that happen again. "We were stupid even trying the first time. We won't do it again. End of discussion."

"Frank, we have do something to draw him out." Lori Anne tore herself from Ben's arms. "We'll bait him but this time with a party celebrating your engagement to Norma."

Ben jumped from his chair, arms still around his wife, her feet dangling. "Don't you think for one second, woman, that you're getting involved in this. I won't let you."

She grinned. "Now you know that won't work with me, you big lug. Shut up and listen. And for goodness sake, put me down."

"This better be good." He grumbled, finally letting her go.

"Charlie's jealous - of you, Frank." She pushed Ben back in the chair.

"Why do you say that?"

"Well, Charlie loved, or thought he loved Norma. And that she loved him. So - if he thinks she has a new love, he just might be jealous enough to want to kill you."

"Oh, that makes me feel better." He tried to laugh. "Then why go after Norma? Why not me?"

Lori Anne put her hand on Frank's shoulder. "Because he's nuts."

"Gotta a point, Sis." Norma polished off the shot of brandy. "Where will we have this party?"

Lori Anne thought for a minute. "Ms. Violet's. She has the room, will love hosting a big party. No need to tell her the real reason."

Bard spoke up. "Have to let the Sheriff and the Chief know."

"Absolutely. Have men stationed around the house." Though Frank still didn't like the idea but didn't have a better one.

"Okay, I'll arrange everything." Lori Anne hugged her husband. "And you, my dear, can dress up in your Sunday best."

"Hell, woman, I'll be the guy who catches this creep, dead or alive."

Somehow Charlie escaped the pond. Norma knew it. She wasn't mistaken. It was Charlie at Lori Anne's house.

CHAPTER THIRTY-ONE

Not being able to do any more about Charlie terrorizing Norma and Lori Anne than putting out an alert for him, Sheriff John Brawley needed solitude, time to think, to sort things out.

He drove to the Spring Grounds, made his way through thick brush to Sunflower Lake, a favorite thinking place for him and the Chief from when they were kids, where they decided to be lawmen, to save the world from evil.

As he sat down on the trunk of a fallen tree, a crisp breeze brushed against his cheek, a familiar, comforting feeling.

The sunflowers usually rimming the lake had gone to sleep for the coming winter, nature caring for her world while humans threatened to destroy theirs.

He sat staring into the water's deepness, the thought of Soft Pond and what it held surfaced.

Who had been in there so long? The coroner's guess was fifty years, maybe more. Chances were the few remains would never be identified. Maybe from the skull. Maybe from DNA. Maybe not.

Were the fires and the discovery at the pond connected? Did someone want attention diverted from the pond?

His mind searched its database. The only person missing for that long was Azalea White. Sheriff Brawley knew Mac had not accepted the theory that she'd run off with her young man. And what about Charlie's body? Could he possibly still be alive?

The rustle of knee-high weeds meant someone coming from behind him.

"Hey, John. Saw your vehicle." Mac sat down next to the Sheriff. "Got some thinking to do myself."

Still gazing at the water, John asked, "You recall the story about the money said to be at the bottom of Soft Pond?"

"Sure. The Indians were paid a lot of money for this land but the Chief was afraid of the money changing his people so he threw it all in the pond. Some say the money is still there."

"Maybe. Wish we'd found it instead of those bodies. And the remains of who knows who that might be."

"Got my own thoughts."

"Figured you did."

The men sat quietly, watching ducks fly overhead.

"Deer season is coming up."

"Two more weeks."

"There'll be trouble. Always some northerner thinks he can hunt on just anybody's property."

"Over a thousand deer were took last year; ten years ago less than five hundred. Either the deer are getting dumber or the hunters are getting sharper."

"Or maybe the bucks are humpin' the ladies more."

"You think the Historical Foundation can ever re-build this place?"

"They sure are trying. It's hard to believe there used to be thousands of visitors every year tramping over these grounds."

"And they came from all over the country."

The surrounding area gave little indication of its once famous reputation.

Gazebos were swallowed by weeds, destroyed by weather or trashed by local kids with nothing better to do.

Bridges crossing slow-running streams, the bath houses, the hotel had long ago disappeared.

"Used to be a boat house over there." Sheriff waved his arm in a vague direction. "Somewhere around here was a huge gazebo. Supposed to have been four times bigger than any of the others. It covered four mineral springs. Took twelve posts to hold it up."

"Wonder if they're still running."

"Don't know. But we better get back.." His head turned. "You hear something?"

Chief MacLoone stood up, listening. "No. Probably a squirrel," he answered, holding out a helping hand to the Sheriff. "Think I'll take a run over to Ms. White's place."

Sheriff Brawley took the hand gratefully, giving out a low moan as he straightened up.

"That knee still giving you trouble?" the Chief asked.

"Afraid so. Chasing that shit head did it in."

"Diving through a window didn't help."

"Damn fool got my Irish up."

"What did he call you?"

"Nothing I care to repeat."

CHAPTER THIRTY-TWO

Frank, afraid to leave Norma, insisted that they both stay at Nell's place. Ben and Lori Anne said they'd be there tomorrow to start planning the party, unless, Ben added, Frank thought they should stay at Nell's, too. Not necessary, Frank told him.

Settled again at Nell's Norma went to work on Grandmother's manuscript but Frank got antsy sitting around, watching the road, walking around the yard. He resisted calling the Two Street Saloon in Phoenix. If he was needed, Aldo would let him know, he kept telling himself. *You're planning on making him a partner because you trust him to take care of things.* The urge grew too strong and he made the call.

"Hey, Aldo. It's Frank. How's it going?"

"Fine, Mr. D. Everything okay?"

"Got a few things to work out. How's your new helper working out?"

"Ernesto? Great. He learns fast, can fix most anything and is a favorite of the customers, teaching some of them Mexican. Mickie set the family up in a nice apartment, hired his daughter to help out at her place in exchange for the rent."

"And the baby?"

"Growing like a weed. Mickie had Ernie - he likes that better than Ernesto - and his daughter get check-ups from her doctor and the kid of course goes to a baby doctor. Mickie had a room at the restaurant set up as a nursery, even hired a sitter. Paid for everything."

"She's quite a gal. How about Karen?"

"She's got it all under control, could use some help, though. Okay if we hire someone part time?"

Frank mulled that over for a moment. "Aldo, how would you feel about being General Manager instead of Maintenance Engineer?"

There was stunned silence at the other end.

"Aldo, you still there?"

"I'm here. Just surprised is all. That would be great, Mr. D."

"You're running the place anyway. Might as well have the title. Means a nice salary increase, more vacation time. And you can make the decisions without asking me."

"Sounds like you're staying in Illinois."

"Sure does, doesn't it? I'm as surprised as you are. Ask Karen to send me a financial statement Federal Express, address it care of Nell Whitaker. Include anything else you think I should see. You know how to reach me. Make sure Karen does, too, just in case."

"Okay, Mr. D. And thanks. I appreciate it."

"You can call me Frank, you know."

"Can't do it. Your dad was Mr. D. and so are you."

"Whatever you say, Also. Now get back to work."

"I'm gone. Bye."

Frank hung up feeling good. He'd thought about making Aldo a partner in the business but his father's instructions to always work alone nixed the idea. Aldo would do great as General Manager.

And dear Mickie Mastrogiuseppe had lived up to her reputation as one classy lady. Ever since Louie DeCani bribed a police officer to spirit her away from Bugsy Siegel under the guise of putting her under protective custody from a rejected government official, she'd never let him or his son down.

Frank knew it couldn't have been easy for his father who was in love with Mickie, never proposed, always hoping that his wife, Teresa, would return. Frank understood. A small part of him still looked for his mother to suddenly appear.

One day when Lori Anne drove over to help Nell with the party plans, Ben went along and soon found work Nell needed done in the barn. Frank thought there must be something he could help with and found Ben behind the barn, watching over a burning pile of rubbish.

The big man said he didn't need help but if Frank wanted to chew the fat for a bit, just sit on that bucket over there by the mower. Turn it over first, though. Frank came back with, "I may be from the city but I do know how to sit on a bucket."

"Just joshin' you, Frank. You're an okay guy."

"Same here. I envy you and Lori Anne." He gazed at the sky, the open fields. "Living out here, away from the noise and crowds, raising your kids. A good life."

"Sure is. I wouldn't, couldn't live any other way. Lori Anne, she's a great gal, gave me great kids. Oh, we have our squabbles but when we go to bed at night, all is forgiven and forgotten." Ben poked at the fire, keeping it within the circle of dirt he'd made. "Course city livin's got its advantages, too."

"How so?"

"Got culture. Libraries, museums, and the like. I tell you, Frank, I'm really looking forward to this trip. Gonna see things I never thought I would. Gonna take pictures of it all."

"Just be careful going through those x-ray machines at the airports. Sometimes they ruin film."

"I thought of that. Gonna buy film over there even if it does cost more and mail it back to be developed. Don't want to take any chances."

"Good idea. I better get back to the house." Frank started to put the bucket back but Ben said, "Just leave it, Frank. I'm about ready to sit a spell myself."

"Okay. See you later." Frank rounded the barn, caught Nell running towards him.

Fighting to catch her breath, Nell panted, "Norma's gone, Frank. The mail came, a letter for Norma. Didn't say where she was going. Took off in the truck like going to a fire."

"You know who it was from?"

"No. She stuck it in her pocket, mad as hell."

"Call the Sheriff. Tell him what happened, alert everyone. Anyone sees, stop her." Whatever was wrong, he'd fix it. Somehow "And call me if you hear anything."

Slamming the Land Rover's gas pedal to the floor he raced down Sailor Springs' Main Street to the road leading to Tricklebanks Tea Room, spotted Nell's truck parked on the road in front, across from the Spring Grounds.

Ignoring the dreaded cow pies, he climbed over the fence, trudged through thick brush toward the precarious wooden steps on the hill.

Norma stood at the top facing the vacant site of the former Glendale Hotel.

Straining to get control of himself, appearing calm, he took a moment before saying, "Hi. What are you - - ?"

She turned, eyes blazing anger, teeth clinched, fists at her sides. "You bastard."

"What the hell?"

"You lied to me. All along you've been lying to me. How dare you! How stupid can I be?"

His heart sank. "What's this all about?"

"Your wife! You son-of-a-bitch liar!" She threw a crumbled envelope at him.

He caught it before it hit the ground. Inside were three marriage certificates. "Norma, - - ."

Her hands went up. "Stop. Don't say one more word. Ever. I can't - will not — listen any more. At least I knew up front Charlie had a wife. The only difference between you and Charlie is you didn't try to kill me. Or was that next?" She screamed, "Get - - out - - of - - my - - life!", whirled around, running, disappearing into the woods.

He stuffed the papers in a pocket. *Sunflower Lake*! Spotting her head bobbing above tall weeds, he dashed up a brush-covered knoll, caught sight of her again, and sliding on slick grass landed almost on top of her. He grabbed her shoulders.

She screamed, a fire storm of anger, kicking, scratching, searching for an opening between his legs.

Down. Get her down. One swift, move trapped flailing arms, a leg coiled around her, forced her to the ground.

"Charlie's my wife!"

Norma stared, motionless, teeth still locked in his sleeve.

"It's my wife riding that motorcycle." His lungs yearned for more air. "I *can* explain."

She sneered, lips curling, eyes narrowed.

"I, Francesco Michele DeCani, swear to tell the truth and nothing but."

His sleeve fell from her teeth. He backed off, waited as she sat up, arms around her knees.

"Can't we go home?" he asked, squatting among the weeds.

She hugged her knees defiantly.

Consigned to adding more dirt to his pants, he squirmed, striving for some semblance of comfort, he until "Okay. Here it is."

CHAPTER THIRTY-THREE

The Sheriff's cell phone sounded first, followed immediately by the Chief's. A hand automatically on his holster, John asked, "Any idea where she went?"

He shook his head at Mac, who told his caller, "We're on it."

A flock of birds rising up out of the trees, chattering wildly, fleeing apparent danger grabbed their attention.

Loud voices, a scream.

John motioned to Mac to take left flank. Guns drawn, they headed where the birds had come from; the other side of the lake. Staying low, John crept through the thick brush. Frank's voice came from nearby.

He stood up slowly, catching sight of Mac appearing above high weeds. John nodded. Guns lowered, they went forward.

Frank sat on the ground in front of Norma, both breathing heavily.

John holstered his gun. "You two doing all that hollering?"

"Everything okay? You don't look so good." Mac wiped sweat from his forehead, swearing to get back in shape.

Resigned to the inevitable, Frank patted a flat space beside him. "Have a seat, gentlemen. I'm attempting to explain to this beautiful woman - - never mind. Just listen. You need to hear my sordid story, too."

"What you think, John?" Mac nudged the Sheriff. "Shall we listen or run them in for wasting a law officer's time?"

"I could use a good story but let's get back to the cars. More comfortable."

Ignoring Frank's outstretched hand, Norma allowed Mac to help her up. She wrestled with the sweater twisted around her, caught Frank watching and quickly turned her back to him, then brushed off what dirt and weeds she could, shook out her hair, and followed Mac.

Frank got ahead to hold open the door of the Sheriff's SUV. Norma, holding Mac's hand as she climbed in, used Frank's foot as if a step stool. No apology offered.

"Okay, Frank. Let's hear it." Arms folded across their chests, the two officers waited.

Frank couldn't remember ever feeling so vulnerable, so helpless. The wrong word, a gesture misread, any little thing could erase whatever chance he had now.

A glance at Norma's face told him she was steeled against any explanation. He had to sound contrite yet truthful. *Here goes.*

Frank stuck his hands in his jacket's pockets, took a deep breath, and began.

He told how he'd met Dawn Dupree, her failed movie career, how she'd help him stay drunk enough to marry her, not only once but three times.

A faint smile appeared on Norma's lips. She quickly squashed it.

Pretending not to have noticed, he told about wanting a divorce, about PeeWee looking for her, calling saying he'd found out she rode a motorcycle with a gold star on each side.

"Bard and I were on our way to Effingham when a motorcycle passed us and I saw a gold star on its side."

He stepped forward, apologized to Norma for the setting, that he'd planned to tell her in a more appropriate place at a more appropriate time, finishing with a simple, "I do love you, Norma. I wanted to tell you but I didn't know how without hurting you. I'm sorry."

She stared at the ground, then at his clothes. "You're a mess."

"Like you're not?" He brushed at weeds clinging to his new Levis. "Now I know why men wear these. Never know when they'll have to run down their women."

Their eyes met. She moved closer. "I'm not running now."

"You are a she-devil when you're mad."

"So don't make me mad."

"Seal the deal with a kiss?"

He didn't let her answer, instead pulled her head to his lips, trailing kisses down to her mouth, taking her lips softly, slowly, until she slid off the seat, melted against him. "Shouldn't we go home?" she whispered.

"You go any further with that it better be at home," chuckled Mac.

The Sheriff joined in. "Yes. I'd hate to have to arrest you for making out in public."

Frank smiled. "Forgot about you. Sorry"

"Oh, that's just great. Ignoring the law. Ought to run you in just for that. What do you think, Mac?"

"Too much paperwork. You two need to go to Nell's, just in case that wife of yours is watching."

The Sheriff opened the car door. "Get in there, both of you."

He took Mac aside. "Sounds like that Dawn woman is really nuts. No telling what she'd do if she caught the two of them alone."

"You're right." The Chief agreed "You get them to Nell's.. "I'll pay Ms. Violet a visit."

"You don't give up, do you?"

"Neither do you, my friend. I still think she had something to do with her sister's disappearance and that she has something to do with the troubles we're having now or she knows who is doing it and why. Maybe I can get a feel for one or the other."

"Okay. Let me know how it goes."

Frank and Norma watched, straining to read their lips.

CHAPTER THIRTY-FOUR

Mac had no jurisdiction outside Olney city limits but when it came to crime there were no boundaries, not in Chief of Police Sean MacLoone's mind. If the crime warranted it, he had no problem dragging a suspect back to town before formally making the arrest. No one complained. No one would believe a criminal.

He approached AzLee's Bed & Breakfast from a back road rarely used by anyone but deer and quail hunters.

Surprised to see Otho's rusty Buick parked at the far side of the house he let the car creep to a stop, then sat quietly, waiting, watching through binoculars.

In a few moments Otho came out of the house, stopping to count a wad of bills. Mac couldn't make out the denominations but Otho seemed quite pleased.

With Otho's car disappearing around the bend, Mac started driving slowly forward, then stopped. Another car coming.

He recognized it as Betty's, from the café. She parked at the foot of the porch steps, looked around and went inside the house. Again he waited.

Time went by. He checked his watch. Needed to get back to the office. The front door opened. He raised the binoculars.

Through the screen door he could see Violet and Betty kissing - on the mouth. Lowering the glasses he took a deep breath and looked again. They were still standing there, Violet rubbing, no, caressing the younger woman's arms. *I'll be damned.* He kept watching until Betty drove off.

Need a cigarette. He'd promised his daughter he'd never touch another smoke. *There's gotta be at least one damn butt in this car.* A quick search turned up nothing except a handwritten note under the front seat, "Forget it, Dad." *Sometimes that girl is too damn smart.*

Minutes went by as he waited for any more surprise guests. No one else appeared. He moved the car towards the house, spying a curtain at the front window closing.

He stepped out of the squad car slowly, giving Ms. White time to move away from the window. After stretching his six foot six frame and twisting the thickening waist to relieve his stiff back, he took porch steps two at a time. Ms. White opened the door just as he reached for the bell.

"Mac," she held her arm across the doorway, blocking his entrance. "What can I do for you today?"

"Thought maybe you'd have some fresh coffee to spare. Stayed too long out at Sunflower Lake and could use some caffeine to get me going again."

He sat down on one of the several white wicker chairs strewn about the wide porch and laid his hat on the matching side table.

"Sure thing, Mac. Be right back."

Mac propped his feet up on the banister.   Folks who knew Azalea well had told him she wasn't the type to run away from home, much less with a man. She wasn't strong-willed, hard like Violet but kind, offering help to anyone who needed it, the first to volunteer for any committee, active in the Baptist Church activities, always had chocolate chip and peanut butter cookies for the town's kids.

Violet returned with a tray holding a mug of hot coffee and a plate of fresh apple slices and banana bread. "Here you go, Mac. Enjoy."

"This is mighty nice of you, Violet." He busied himself with a slice of apple.

"What were you doing at the Lake?"

"Had some thinking to do." He sipped on the hot coffee. "You hear about the findings at Soft Pond?"

"You know I did. News spreads quick around here."

"Know anything you'd like to share?"

"Don't dance around me with your nasty little suspicions, Mac." Her aging eyes twinkled yet he saw only evil in them.

"Now don't go jumping to conclusions." His mouth went into a one-sided grin.

"And don't try that sardonic smile on me, Chief MacLoone. Doesn't matter what you think. Nobody knows what happened to my sister. Nobody ever will. She disappeared years and years ago."

"About fifty, right?"

"Yes, I buried her, " she arched an eyebrow at him, "in my heart, long ago."

He took his time finishing off a slice of the bread and the coffee. "I inherited this case and just can't give up on it."

At the car he leaned casually on its roof. "Don't you worry about it, Violet. I'll find her. Someday. That's a promise."

Violet didn't respond. She wanted to get back to her room, her sanctuary, her haven.

Business required she be lenient with her guests, bending to their petty little whims, but in her own room life was as she wanted it.

Once a week Elsie came from her job at the Olney Motel to clean, do the laundry, the ironing. She had full access to the house except for Ms. Violet's room. Violet and only Violet tended to it.

Sheets on the double bed were washed every Monday and put back on the bed straight from the dryer, never changing them until paper thin and torn. Her record for one set of sheets was seven years.

Tuesday was ironing day, though usually that involved only the pillow cases. She liked smooth pillow cases.

Wednesdays she sat down at the desk in the room next to her bedroom, did the bookkeeping, paid bills, deposited checks from guests, withdrew funds from a money market account when needed.

Thursday she planned meals for the following week and did the shopping.

Her entertainment was shopping, finding which store had the best prices on the needed items. No matter there were only two supermarkets in town. If a store within a twenty-mile radius had a good sale she made it into a day trip, especially if it was in Effingham where she could get her hair done at the beauty school. Otherwise she took care of it herself on Friday.

Saturday she puttered around the house and yard, making herself available to guests in the event some wanted to do nothing but sit around and visit. That left her mind free to think of new ways to advertise her business.

Sundays she went for a leisurely drive, visiting friends, checking out yard sales, always passing slowly by Soft Pond.

+ + + + +

Mac used the drive back to Olney to absorb what he'd just discovered at AzLee's B&B. Betty and Violet. Now wasn't that something.

Funny that someone as secretive as Violet would seek out the town gossip. Or had Betty initiated the intimate relationship? Didn't really matter.

What did matter was that if Betty knew a thing she liked telling it. Would she know what was up with Otho and Violet? Maybe.

He called John. If he was going to be in his office for a while okay if he stopped by? Putting down his cell phone he turned the car towards Louisville.

CHAPTER THIRTY-FIVE

Nell couldn't believe her eyes when Frank and Norma stepped out of Sheriff Brawley's car clothes dirty, disheveled. "You two been in a fight?" she held the front door open.

With sly smiles at each other, they said in unison, "Yep."

"Well, get in here. I'll make some Irish coffee while you get cleaned up. Frank, you'll find my husband's clothes still in the hall closet. Norma, look in my closet. Must be something that'll do for the moment. Now get upstairs, both of you. I'll tell Bard you're here."

"Where is he?"

"In the kitchen, Frank. Making calls, trying to get someone to write an article about Sailor Springs"

"That's great."

"Now git!"

"Yes, ma-am." Norma saluted, following Frank up the stairs.

Nell shouted, "And no fooling around. I have to hear this story. It must be a doozie."

+ + + + +

Tired and dirty, they wanted hot showers and clean clothes. Frank tried to get in the shower with her, but Norma pushed him out and locked the door.

He waited patiently, enjoying her singing through the running water. What about Dawn? Even if she did get caught, that didn't guarantee she'd give him the divorce. Maybe if he offered her - what? Money? No. She already had plenty of that. Role in a movie? How could he do that? Bard might have connections.

And where in the hell was Charlie's body? Who would steal a body? Why? And the fires. And let's not forget about those remains found in the pond. So much for the quiet country life.

Norma opened the bathroom door, steam spilling out around her. "God, that felt good."

Frank grinned. "Why don't you take off that towel and come over here, pretty lady."

She wrapped the towel tighter around her, accenting every curve.

"No way. You get in there, wash yourself off and take long enough for me to get dressed and skedaddle down stairs before you're out."

"Am I forgiven?" He stood up, waited for her to come to him.

Instead, she walked to the closet. "Yes. But let's not talk about that now."

"Okay. See you downstairs."

"Frank." She turned around. "I do love you and I trust you."

He started towards her but she held up her hand. "No. Not now. I'm tired and confused. I just wanted you to know."

"That's all I want, for you to believe." He blew a kiss to her and obediently went for the shower.

+ + + + +

By the time he got downstairs Norma and Nell were in the parlor enjoying the spiked coffee.

"Where's Bard?" he asked.

"Still in the kitchen. I've told Nell what happened at the lake." Norma watched a wave of relief flow over Frank's face. She'd saved him having to repeat it.

"Good." He took the welcome drink Nell offered and sat beside Norma on the couch.

"Why didn't you go back to the B&B? Not that I mind having you here. You know you're always welcome." Nell looked from one to the other for an answer. "Well?"

Norma wasn't sure whether or not to mention the conversation between the Sheriff and Chief MacLoone.

She looked at Frank and, as though reading her thoughts, he said, "John thought we might be in danger there if Dawn saw us together, that we'd be safe here. After we were in John's SUV, he and Mac walked off a ways to talk. We couldn't hear what they said but with a little lip-reading could tell it was about Violet and her sister's disappearance."

"And Mac not giving up. I caught the word 'fires'', too." Norma added.

"You two are pretty good at reading lips, aren't you?" Nell finished her drink, refilled her cup. "Ready for another?"

"One more," Norma held out her cup, waited until Nell filled it. "I've had a lot of practice, research, you know. Comes in handy when you can't get close enough to hear."

"She's a woman of many talents." Frank took one more slug of coffee and poured himself another. "This is great stuff, Nell. Thanks."

"Bet you're feeling better."

"Sure am. You must know Violet well, probably all you life, right?"

"Don't think anyone knows her very well. She keeps mostly to herself, especially since her sister's been gone. Her opening the B&B surprised everyone but apparently it's worked out. I do know that Mac has suspected all along that Violet knows more than she says about Azalea.

"She's friendly but seems to have a wall built, keeps people from getting close." Norma said, "It's probably why Violet had picked the house outside of town and off the main road for her business. "Doesn't show her emotions. Women her age usually develop laugh lines, creases from frowning but not her."

"Just lucky?" Nell shrugged.

"Whatever, we won't find out anything sitting here. Wish Bard would get in here."

Frank stiffened at the golden flecks in her eyes sparkling with excitement. "What do you mean? Find out what?"

"There's something going on around here and I want to know what it is. Don't you?"

Frank just stared at her.

She asked Nell, "Aren't you curious? Someone is setting fires, a body is missing, a movie star is running around on a motorcycle."

"Sure but I'm only concerned about your safety, yours and Frank's."

Frank spoke up. "She's not a movie star, just an actress, and not a very good one."

Norma's voice rose a few octaves. "At least we know it's not Charlie!"

"Okay. You got me there. Happy?"

"Yes." She patted his knee. "Felt good, too."

Nell broke in. "Let's concentrate on your engagement party, shall we?"

"Wait a minute. Where's Lori? My sister has to be part of this. It was her idea."

"They're in their way. I called them while you were upstairs."

A ruckus out front interrupted her. "Must be Lori and Ben. I'll open the gate."

As soon as Nell was out of the house Frank took Norma by the shoulders. "You aren't thinking of snooping around, are you? Perhaps for your next book?"

"It's called research, darling. After the party and what's-her-name is caught, which I am sure she will be, then we'll see what we can find."

"You're including me?"

"Of course." She kissed his nose. "You don't want me out there all alone, do you?"

He concentrated on her lips. "Shut up, woman." They didn't hear the others coming in the house.

"You can stop now. We're here," shouted Lori Anne from the doorway. She rushed over to her sister. "You okay?"

"I'm fine. Really."

Ben slapped Frank on the back. "Hear you won the battle."

"I'm not so sure about that." Frank stood up. "Now will one of you talk some sense into her? She wants to investigate the fires, the missing body, everything."

"Sounds like fun to me," grinned Lori Anne.

"Thanks, Sis." Norma hooked her arm onto Frank's. "He's agreed to help us."

"Under duress, may I add."

"Surely Bard is finished with those phone calls. I'll get him." Nell started towards the kitchen just as Bard came down the hall. He wrapped an arm around her waist. "What's Frank doing under duress?"

"Something I think we'll all get involved in."

CHAPTER THIRTY-SIX

Like other Illinois counties, Clay County was dotted with farms long-deserted, outbuildings time-worn, weather-beaten, steadily returning to the earth.

Between Olney and Sailor Springs birds nesting in the barn of one such farm were disturbed by a motorcycle's motor. It's grinding noise stopped, the birds returned.

Below the rafters the bike's rider pulled off her helmet, shook out the short, copper-dyed curls, tore off the heavy black leather jacket and tossed it aside. Something slipped from one of the pockets. Oh, yes, she sneered. The family photo.

Picking it up from the hay-covered floor, she sat down on a rusted kitchen stool.

Probably left by that doofus of a kid. What was his name? Something stupid. Otho. That was it. Said everyone called him 'O'. Now how stupid was that!

The picture brought memories flooding back. How old was she then? Maybe six, seven years old. She and a little boy, about the same age, she guessed, were standing in front of a man at a beach. Mama had told her the man was her uncle, the boy her cousin. She never saw them again.

Later when Mama was dying she told Dawn the man was really her father, the boy her half-brother. His name was Chuck. There was another boy, older than Chuck. His name was Bard. He hadn't made the trip from Illinois to California.

They were so very young back then. Had Chuck remembered her? She thought not. The male beast had such a bad memory, forgetting things like anniversaries, birthdays, phone calls, a wife. Her many marriages had taught her well.

When her mother told her about the boys, she remarked how Dawn could have been Chuck's twin. The picture in the paper proved they still looked alike so many years later. The only apparent difference being the color of hair, his a bright copper-color, her's a warm brown., sable she called it.

The private detective she'd hired to find out more about Chuck was young but highly recommended by a good friend who said he could find anyone and did. Chuck Bolden had been known in Phoenix Arizona as Charlie Doyle, had done very well as a stock broker but his personal life was a sham.

He beat his wife, cheated on her constantly, was often in therapy for a mental disorder. Charlie died in a swamp, an accident, the newspaper reported, no will, one sibling, a brother, Bard Bolden Doyle. She wanted to know more. Her friend found the answers.

Bard was in Illinois, with his college friend, Frank DeCani, planning to open a bed and breakfast near Olney. Frank had seen a lawyer about divorcing Dawn, left his restaurant in Phoenix to be with his girl friend in Sailor Springs.

She wondered if Chuck, too, had suffered from deep depressions and exhilarating highs. He'd have loved the highs as she did, conveniently forgetting to take the necessary medication in order to enjoy life to the fullest.

Like roaring out of the city into the countryside on her top-of-the-line Kawasaki sports model ZX=6R 636CC, gold stars on the lower cowlings announcing to the world she was still a star. Armed with saddle bags of military ready-to-eat meals She soared up mountains, through deep woods of California, Oregon, Washington State, queen of all she surveyed, stopping wherever she wanted to eat or sleep, needing no one. Pure freedom.

Afterwards came the heavy depression. It began slowly, sneaking into her mind with reminders of the evil soul lurking there, bringing on a deep sadness, pulling her into the depths of hell. She knew the signs well and fought them off until finding a safe place to crash for however long it took, sometimes days, even weeks. Pills let her sleep through most of it.

Now little Chuck was dead. Whatever happened had nothing to do with Dawn Dupree DeCani. What fun to be dead. Crazy fun.

CHAPTER THIRTY-SEVEN

The Clay County Weekly newspaper announced Frank and Norma's engagement, invitations of a party hosted by Ms. Violet were sent. Word quickly spread as Olney Catering prepared the menu carefully chosen by Lori Anne and Nell.

Norma promised she'd stay out of the way, spending the time on Grandma's manuscript.

Flowers from the Olney florist were argued over, the local musicians Ms. Violet always used for special occasions were scheduled, extra tables and chairs were provided by a generous rental company.

The Sheriff's men planned the ambush.

The morning of the party Norma woke with a jolt. Tonight 'Charlie' would be caught. Then what? She punched her pillow into a soft lump, tucked it under her head and turned to the man sleeping beside her, only to be greeted by the smile that never failed to beguile her.

"Morning, Glory." He raised the sheet, pulling it over them. "I love you."

"And I love you, Mr. DeCani."

"Mr. DeCani needs Mrs. DeCani."

"Not yet. This is only an affair."

He nuzzled her neck. "You know what an affair means, don't you?"

She moved against him. "Yes, forbidden, illicit sex between two horny, unfaithful human beings"

"Yeah," he growled, lips reaching hers, hands cupping her breasts, teasing hard nipples. Her breathing quickened, chest heaving as he slowly, knowingly seduced her body, her mind.

CHAPTER THIRTY-EIGHT

Party day was filled with last minute details. The women made one last run to Ms. Violet's and visits to the beauty shop.

Frank, Ben, and Bard, having gotten haircuts a few days before and picking up their suits at the dry cleaners, didn't have much to do. Luckily they all liked football as it was the only game on TV.

Lori Anne made sandwiches and left a good supply of snacks before going into town.

Beer was not provided as no one wanted men smelling of liquor and the belching that went with it.

In late afternoon Lori Anne, Nell, and Norma returned. They came in the back door, laughing and chatting about their day and the evening festivities. Never mind the reason for the party. It was a party and they were making the most of it.

A pleasant surprise waited in the parlor.

The three men, in their suits, white shirts, real ties, not the snap-on kind, handkerchiefs folded properly with only two points showing, each holding a corsage for their date.

"Good gravy, would you look at this?" Lori Anne circled Ben. "Even your shoes are shined!"

"Yes, ma-am."

Nell dropped her packages. "Look at that hand-kerchief! Just like in the movies."

Bard covered the few steps between them, handed her the corsage, then withdrew a small, black velvet box. Down on one knee, he took her hand, opened the box, offered it up to her. "Ms. Nell, I love you with all my heart. Will you marry me?"

Her free hand flew to her mouth, her face turning bright pink. "Oh! Oh!"

"Please?"

She didn't answer.

"Pretty please with sugar on it?"

That brought the widest smile ever seen on her usually stoic face. "Yes! Of course! Yes!"

"Whoopee!" screamed Lori Anne.

"Holy cat fish!" Norma grabbed Nell, Lori Anne joined in hugging the bride-to-be until she pleaded for mercy.

Then they ran for Bard, repeating their reaction. When he was able to escape, Norma turned on Frank.

"I suppose you knew about this days ago."

Hands up, he surrendered. "Guilty. But for a good cause. He wanted it to be a surprise."

"And you, my dear husband," Lori Anne stood in front of Ben, hands on hips, "Did you know, too?"

"Whoa, woman. I wanted to tell you, honest, but I was outnumbered. Right, guys?" He stared at Frank and Bard. "Help me out here."

"We threatened to take him out behind the barn." Frank put up his fists.

Lori Anne sneered. "You two wouldn't have a chance against this big lute."

"Okay, okay." Norma took center stage. "We're just so happy for the two of you. That's great." She winked at Nell. "Tell you what. We'll throw you an even bigger engagement party when this masquerade is over tonight."

Bard hugged Nell, "Maybe we'll skip the engagement and go right to the wedding? How's that sit with you, Ms. Nell?"

She took her time answering, looking around at the others, down at the floor, making him wait, finally s aying, "That sits just fine with me, Mr. Bard."

"And now, gentlemen," Lori Anne interrupted, "if you will excuse us, we must get beautiful." She and Norma fled upstairs while Nell with one last kiss from Bard disappeared into her room.

+ + + + +

Nell appeared first in pearl-grey silk slacks, matching tunic with pearl necklace and earrings. "I haven't worn anything like this in years. Feel like a kid playing dress-up."

Bard whistled. "Sure beats those bib overalls you cotton to."

As he wrapped his arms around her, Lori Anne yelled from the top of the stairs, "Here we come!"

Her street-length dress was a shimmering sky-blue, tear drops of crystal circled her neck and dripped from her earlobes. "What you think, Ben?"

"Lordy, lordy, God have mercy."

"I take it that's good?"

"More than good, woman. You are down right awesome."

Norma followed behind wearing a simple black sleeveless sheath, white squirrel broach at her shoulder, the matching earrings showing from under auburn curls.

Frank walked over to the staircase, held out his hand, "My queen."

She laid her hand in his. "You approve, my King?"

"Oh, yes, milady. Very definitely yes."

CHAPTER THIRTY-NINE

Arriving at AzLee's Bed & Breakfast the three couples were surprised to find it already filled with invited guests and some uninvited but no one complained, more witnesses for whatever happened

Sheriff's men were stationed in the woods along side the front road approaching the house with a couple of the Chief's men watching the only back road.

The autumn night had turned colder than usual, banning any outdoor activities. Inside the house a violinist stood in front of the small orchestra, songs of love floated throughout the rooms. Bard started the celebration by offering a toast to the happy couple.

He held a champagne glass. "I think I can speak for all of us that we're glad they are finally making their public displays of affection legal."

The room broke into laughter. "Hear, hear!" several yelled.

Frank, holding Norma's hand, stepped forward. "Keep your glasses up, ladies and gentlemen. We have another engagement to celebrate." Motioning to Nell and Bard, he said, "I'm happy to be the first to tell you that just today Bard proposed to Nell and she said - YES!"

Gasps of surprise were followed by women surrounding Nell, men slapping Bard on the back and shaking his hand in congratulations.

The Chief yelled, "A toast! To Norma and Frank, To Nell and Bard!"

Wine glasses were held high, the orchestra began playing. Couples began swaying with the music, wives pulled reluctant husbands towards the dance floor, unattached girls giggled as young men approached cautiously, fearing rejection.

Suddenly the music, the laughter paled, paralyzed by a thundering roar from the back of the house; the kitchen door exploding, a motorcycle racing down the hallway, crisscrossing through rooms, guests screaming, scrambling for the front door, escaping up the staircase.

The danger vanished out through the kitchen into the deep woods. Stunned, families began gathering together, friends searched for each other.

Mac and John helped those who had tripped, fallen to the floor while yelling for their men.

"Check if anyone's hurt."

"Anyone see where it came from?"

"Where did it go? What direction?"

A voice rose above the noise. "Get a doctor!"

The crowd surged towards the voice. On the floor of the parlor, among broken furniture, spilled food, lay Ms. Violet. John pushed his way forward, felt her pulse, listened at her mouth. "She's alive. May be a heart attack" Mac was already on his cell.

Within minutes a siren was heard, paramedics arrived. The crowd stepped aside, giving them space. Ms. Violet being tended to, the lawmen debriefed their men.

The motorcycle hadn't come by the front or back road, but from Ms. Violet's storage shed set away from the house.

By the time deputies realized what was happening, it was too late. Paramedics carried Ms. Violet to the ambulance. Slowly, quietly folks returned to their cars.

Lori Anne and Ben found the engaged couples sitting on the porch steps.

"Everybody okay?" Lori Anne put her arm around Norma.

"We're fine." Nell assured her with a weak smile, feeling for her engagement ring, finding it still there. "You sure throw a hell of a party."

"Well, at least it's one folks won't forget." Bard held her closer. "Now what, Frank?"

Frank examined his Brioni suit, stained with wine and mishmash of smorgasbord, breast pocket torn, silk handkerchief gone, slacks ripped.

He automatically thought of Peewee. He'd know how to handle the situation. Remembering the thugs he'd bring in, the thought was quickly dismissed. "I don't know. I just don't know."

Norma stood up, pieces of broken potato chips falling from her hair.

"We ought to see about getting this place cleaned up and check on Ms. Violet."

"We ought to clean ourselves first." Lori Anne started to get up, then fell back down. "Oh, hell."

"Lori Anne!" Ben had never heard his sweet wife swear other than 'Darn.'

"I fell over something, couldn't see what it was, must have twisted my ankle."

Ben picked up her foot. "It's swelling."

"I'll find some ice, make a cold pack. Maybe there's some tape in one of the bathrooms to wrap it." Norma reached for the purse she'd managed not to lose in the chaos. "There's aspirin in here somewhere." She handed it to Lori Anne. "Here. I'll get some water."

Frank suggested instead of making the drive back home they stay there for the night. Ms. Violet wouldn't care. Meanwhile they'd arrange for a clean-up crew and check on her tomorrow.

Ben said his wife couldn't make it up those stairs.

Norma told them to take Ms. Violet's room, the only bedroom downstairs, she and Frank would use his room while Bard and Nell took hers.

Lori Anne's nature was to clean and started hobbling around the kitchen.

Ben told her to stop fussing. She finally gave in, letting Ben carry her into Ms. Violet's room and the others headed upstairs looking forward to hot showers.

+ + + + +

The next day Lori Anne's ankle kept her confined to sitting with the injured foot elevated, keeping the ice pack on ten minutes, off ten minutes.

Spotting a typist chair at the desk in Ms. Violet's office just off the bedroom Lori Anne hopped her way to it. With wheels she'd be able to go through the house, at least the ground floor.

On top of the desk was a monthly calendar spread open, notations written in a type of shorthand. Some began with a "F", some with an "N".

Others bore the initials "F to E", with date and time. "F & N - S.S." date, time. "F & N in" date, time, "F & N out" same date, hours later.

Curious, she slid the top drawer open. Inside lay a black notebook. A quick look through the doorway. No one nearby. Careful not to disturb pens, paper clips in a small tray, she raised the notebook, placed it carefully on the desk. With one finger she lifted the cover. A blank sheet. Using the same finger she turned the page. Then another and another, reading Ms. Violet's clear, precise handwriting.

She heard Norma calling her. "Hey, sis, where are you?"

"In here."

Norma stepped in the room, dragging a filled garbage bag. "What are you - - ?" The look on Lori Anne's face stopped her.

"You won't believe this."

"Lori Anne, you shouldn't be going through Ms. Violet's things." Her eyes followed Lori Anne's finger pointing to entries about "F" and "N", dates, times, events. "Is that who I think it is?"

"You and Frank. Ms. Violet has kept impeccable records on every guest from the time she opened this place until yesterday morning."

"Give me that thing." Norma sat on the desk. "Have you looked in the other drawers?"

Lori Anne grinned. "Now I am."

In the next drawer, deeper than the other, were small photo albums.

Norma put her hand on Lori Anne's. "Make certain those get put back exactly as you found them."

"Gotcha." Lori Anne handed some to Norma. The room grew silent as they each turned page after page of snapshots, Ms. Violet's guests in their rooms, at the dining room table, in the garden out back, on the front lawn, with names, dates, times.

Not needing to ask, Lori Anne pulled open the two drawers on the other side of the desk. The top one held nothing but a checkbook and bills to be paid. The second were more albums, photos of Ms. Violet and her sister, Azalea, intimate pictures.

In one album were a few pictures, these of Ms. Violet and Betty, much like those with her twin.

No one spoke, only startled glances at each other as they traded albums.

After long, silent minutes, Norma put down the album. "Whew. I don't know what to do." Norma slid off the desk. "As bad as all this is, it really isn't any of our business."

"No," Lori Anne agreed.

"You'd think Ms. Violet would have kept the drawers locked."

"Nobody, not even Elsie, the cleaning lady, was allowed in her private rooms. And she kept the doors locked."

Norma's eyebrows went up.

"No, I didn't try the doors. Elsie did, when Ms. Violet was outside."

Just then they heard, "Anybody here?"

There was no mistaking the high-pitched, little-girl voice.

"Cripes." Norma hurried to the door. "Get this stuff back where it was." She shut the door behind her, calling out, "I'm coming."

Still in her party dress from last night, Betty started down the hall but Norma stopped her with a big hug while turning her around.

"Hi, Betty. Sorry the party didn't turn out quite as we'd planned."

"That's okay. By the way, congratulations. And to Nell, too. Tell her for me?"

"Sure. Did you want something?" Norma moved towards the front door, an arm still around Betty's shoulder.

"Stayed at the hospital with Violet most of the night."

Noticing she didn't call her 'Ms. Violet' as most people did, she said. "How is she doing?"

"Doc says it wasn't a heart attack. Must have been overcome by shock, her house being almost demolished, her precious antiques destroyed. But she'll be out in a couple days. They want to keep her under observation. You know how that goes."

"Well, thank you for stopping by. Let her know we'll have this place cleaned up in no time."

Hanging back, trying to see further into the house, Betty said, "We're good friends and I know how persnickety she is. Maybe I can help, know where most things go."

Norma fought back the laugh creeping into her throat. She held the front door open. "That's not necessary, Betty. You have a job to get to and the guys are helping so everything is under control."

Smiling, Betty left, saying as she reached her car, "Call if you need anything."

Norma just smiled back and waved, not moving until Betty's car was out of sight.

"She gone?" Lori Anne asked, hobbling to the door, using a baseball bat as a crutch. "That voice drives me crazy."

"Yes, finally. Let's not say anything to anyone, not even Nell, at least not yet. And where did you find the bat?"

"Under the bed."

"Where is Nell?"

"She had to get back to the farm, feed the animals. She'll be here later."

As they started to the back of the house the crunch of gravel announced another visitor.

"Now who?" Norma pulled back a curtain from the front window. "It's John, the Sheriff."

"Bet Mac is just - - -." Lori Anne stepped out onto the porch. "Yep, here he comes."

The sisters waited as John and Mac parked their SUVs.

"Good morning, ladies." The men chorused.

"Morning, yourselves. What are you two up to this early?"

"Figured you'd start cleaning and wanted another look around before anything was disturbed." John pulled out a notebook.

Mac explained, avoiding using Frank's wife's name. "Maybe we missed something last night, like where the motorcyclist is hiding out."

After everyone had gone to bed and Frank was sound asleep, Norma had crept downstairs, tried to follow the motorcycle's path through the house. She prided herself on picking up on clues to crimes but had found nothing. "Want to share this idea?"

Getting a nod from Mac, John asked, "You haven't vacuumed or swept up yet, have you?"

"No. Wanted to get everything picked up first." Norma told him.

Mac stepped inside the house, holding the door open. "Where're your men?"

Lori Anne glanced at Norma, answered "Ben's seeing if he can fix the screen door in the kitchen."

"Frank and Bard are at the side of the house getting up glass on the lawn from broken windows." Norma told them.

John joined Mac, told the women, "You go around the outside of the house, tell them we're here and not to come in until we say so." The worry line between his eyes deepened. The situation had taken a dangerous turn.

"Will do, John." With an arm around Norma's shoulder and struggling with the bat, Lori Anne took a step and gave out a small yelp.

"Come here, little one." John easily picked her up.

Lori Anne, grinning like a Cheshire cat, put her arms around his neck. "Every cloud has a silver lining."

Mac said, "I'll start at the front and you take the back, John."

"Got it."

Around the corner of house they almost ran into Ben who'd heard his wife's cry.

"What happened?" He held out his arms and John obediently handed her over.

"She tried walking." Seeing Lori Anne safe, securely cuddled in her husband's arms, Norma felt a pang of envy.

John explained again that they had to stay out of the house until he and Mac were through with their investigation. The men obediently returned to their work.

As soon as the Sheriff was inside the kitchen, Norma whispered to Lori Anne, "Let's find you a window where you can see the dining room, it's about in the middle of the house."

Lori Anne whispered back, "Is this what you do when you're for a story, spy on the cops?"

Norma nodded, "Sometimes."

Helping her co-conspirator get settled at the chosen window, Norma moved from window to window, following the Sheriff and the Chief of Police as they went from room to room, heads down, stopping only to pick up something and put in the small paper bag each man carried.

The search ended at the back door, the lawmen coming out, holding the little brown bags.

"Any of you know what these are?" Mac held his bag open.

"Sure do."

"Me, too."

"Of course."

"Why?"

"No."

"Don't have rabbits in the city, that it, Frank?" Mac teased.

"Take a look at these." John offered, holding out the bag he carried. "Rabbit pellets."

"That mean something?" Ben asked.

"Maybe." John turned his attention to the yard. Motioning to Mac to follow and the others to stay put, he walked slowly towards the storage shed. Inside he shined his flashlight around the dirt floor. More rabbit pellets.

DARK SECRETS   -227-

Once outside the shed, he told the group that had followed despite his orders not to, "Ms. Violet didn't have rabbits. She hated them, always getting in her garden."

The group waited for him to explain..

"Come on. I want to show you something."

Ben carried Lori Anne and followed as the others paraded around the house to the front lawn, to John's vehicle.

From the back seat he took a burlap bag. "Mac and I scoured the area where we tracked the motorcycle into the woods and found this with rabbit pellets. Apparently the driver," he ignored Norma and Frank's stares, "arrived with the bag, let the pellets scatter through the house for whatever reason we may never know, then discarded it before escaping."

Mac added, "Lots of people keep rabbits around here. Finding out where these came from may be impossible. But we'll give it a try."

Norma's eye for detail caught a look between the two lawmen, something they weren't saying.

"We have to get back but we'll be in touch." Mac winked. "Have fun getting this place in order."

"Thanks a lot." Norma winked back.

CHAPTER FORTY

Norma was right about there being something she and the others weren't being told.

Mac had remembered that Otho Helmutt used a barn on a deserted farm far out of town to raise rabbits to sell because Betty wouldn't let him have them in her back yard.

He found Otho, asked if anyone had been to the barn besides himself.

The young man said a real good-looking redheaded woman had come to him one day when he was feeding the critters, wanted to rent the place. Offered to pay one thousand dollars for a couple of weeks. A thousand bucks! And the woman said she'd tend to the rabbits so he wouldn't have to bother. How could he turn that down? He didn't tell his aunt. She'd expect him to pay rent.

Did the woman say why she wanted the place? John had asked him. Otho said she was writing a movie script, needed absolute peace and quiet to finish it.

Promised she'd try to write in a small part for him. Imagine, him in a movie!

Leaving Mac to watch after things, Sheriff John Brawley drove to the barn in late afternoon. If Dawn Dupree DeCani was holed up there, she might be getting ready for a night run.

The only clue to the land once being a working farm was the barn. Leaning precariously, John couldn't fathom why it hadn't fallen. Some things, like some people, just never gave up. He appreciated that, honored it.

Stepping inside, the Sheriff's eyes adjusted to the shadows. Pigeons cooed softly from rafters above. He peered through the dimness, venturing slowly past empty stalls, a child's wagon, a milking stool. Toward the back were Otho's rabbit hutches, rabbits of various colors and sizes. Business must be booming.

He started to take a closer look when a flash of light caught his eye.

Approaching cautiously he saw a metallic-blue motorcycle resting against the rusted remains of a tractor. On its side was a gold star.

Something crunched under his foot. He picked up an empty box marked "MRE Chicken & Rice." Near it was another, "MRE Turkey Breast." From his short time in the Army he'd learned the ready-to-eat meals weren't bad eating when on bivouac..

A shuffling sound came from a pile of hay.

"Hey, Sheriff." A muted voice rose from the heap.

He knelt down. A woman with copper-colored hair, outfitted in black leather, her eyes half-closed, a bottle of vodka on her chest. She wiggled a ring-bearing finger at him.

"Dawn DeCani?" he asked, picking up an empty pill bottle at her side.

"The one and - - ." She raised the bottle to her pale lips. Taking what looked like only a few crops, she finished with, "and only." The bottle slipped from her hand, rolling away.

John sat down beside her. "You okay?"

She didn't seem to hear him. "Have to get off the high. Too high this time."

He reached for her wrist, feeling for her pulse. "You need a doctor."

"No, no, Sheriff." Her eyelids flickered. "I'll be okay. Always okay. Just too beautiful, too talented for my - - my own - - good." She attempted a smile. "Me, actress."

A piece of folded paper stuck out of a pocket on her jacket. He leaned closer, lightly withdrew the paper. "You write this?"

No response.

"Dawn?"

He felt her pulse again, put his ear to her mouth. Nothing. He read the note again.

"The body must be destroyed so the soul can be cured."

CHAPTER FORTY-ONE

Frank and the others were finishing up at Ms. Violet's when his cell rang. A few minutes later he called everyone into the kitchen.

"Please - sit down." He told them, waiting until they were seated around the table. "That was the Sheriff. He found - ." Frank glanced at Norma, trying to apologize with his eyes.

She caught his meaning and smiled.

He started again. "John found Dawn. She's been hiding out in a barn on a deserted farm." He hesitated before saying, "She's dead. Apparently suicide, pills and alcohol."

Lori Anne took Norma's hand.

"Thank God that's over." Ben patted Frank's back.

Bard and Nell hugged each other.

Frank got down on one knee in front of Norma, took her left hand in his.

"My lady, will you allow me to replace this ring of opals with one of diamonds? Will you marry me, be my queen, Lady Guinevere?"

Surrounded by the others waiting breathlessly, Norma stroked his face. "Yes, my king. Yes a thousand times over."

"Hot damn!" yelled Ben.

Lori Anne grabbed her sister, pulling her to her feet. "Hot damn double!"

Nell joined Lori Anne and Norma while the men slapped backs, shook hands, laughing at the women jumping and hugging around the room.

Tired of waiting for them to quiet down Frank snatched Norma away. "Anybody mind if I kiss my bride-to-be?"

Taking her in his arms, looking down at her face, flushed, eyes bright, lips waiting to be kissed, he whispered, "Mrs. DeCani."

"Yes, Mr. DeCani?"

"Let's go upstairs."

"Sir!" She tried to pull away. "Not before the wedding."

He swept her up in his arms. "I am king. My wish is your command."

Her arms around his neck, she purred. "At least this time, my king."

"Whoopee!" yelled Ben, the others clapping loudly as Frank carried her upstairs.

CHAPTER FORTY-TWO

After calling the Coroner's Office and seeing Dawn's body was on the way to the morgue, John called Frank, then Mac's office. "Got time for a talk, privately?"

"Sure, John. In twenty minutes?"

"Thanks."

No need to say more. The one place they wouldn't be overheard was Bill's workroom, the morgue.

+ + + + +

Funerals were over for Charlie's victims, the morgue's only occupant Dawn DuPree DeCani resting quietly on a steel tray in a cool drawer.

Though it meant trouble, Bill Hawkins was glad to see the two official vehicles drive around to the back of the building, hear his friends coming in the back door. "What's up, guys?"

John opened the bag he'd carried in, handed it to Mac. "What do you make of this?"

Mac pulled out a pair of black goggles, held them up to the light. "Scuba divers use these. They're scratched, on the side.". He passed them on to Bill. "Where'd you find them?"

"In the barn." John filled Mac in where he'd been, what he found. "Woman's a dead - no pun intended - ringer for Charlie, I mean Chuck. Must be a cousin or maybe half-sister. Know his father played around a lot. After you left, Bill, I took another look around. Found these near Dawn's motorcycle. At first I figured they were her's but they're too thick, too heavy."

Bill put them on. "Prescription glasses."

"Either of you know if Otho Helmutt wears glasses?"

"Contact lenses. Saw him buying lens cleaner at the drugstore." Bill reached for the wall phone, called the only optometrist in Flora. When he hung up, he nodded. "Yep. Contacts. 'O' asked him to make new lens for divers goggles. His old ones were scratched. Doesn't wear the contacts when snorkeling."

"Kid's always looking for ways to make money. Somebody paid him to do it, get Charlie's body from the pond, hide it somewhere." John shook his head. "Still have to find that body."

Mac spoke up. "Remember I told you about seeing him at Ms. Violet's, counting out quite a wad when he left her house?"

"I'll pick him up, Mac. He doesn't know I've been out there, just think I have more questions."

"I want to question him, John, especially about his connection with Ms. Violet."

"One more thing." The Sheriff took a photo from his pocket, handed it to Mac.

Bill leaned over Mac's shoulder. "What this?"

"Found it with Dawn. Look at the back. It's Dawn, her father, and Charlie when he was still Chuck. Taken in California."

"Damn." Mac grunted. "Dawn was Bard's half sister. Sure hate to tell him this if he doesn't already know."

CHAPTER FORTY-THREE

Otho didn't give the Sheriff any trouble when asked to go with him to the Police Station. All he'd done as far as anyone knew was rent out that old barn that didn't belong to anybody. No harm in that.

Sitting in a windowless room at the Olney Police Station, he quickly realized this had nothing to do with renting the barn or the woman writing a secret movie script. Chief MacLoone told him right up front he wasn't being charged with anything, not yet. He'd seen him coming out of Ms. Violet's house, seen him counting a wad of bills. What did she pay him for?

"Did some yard work."

"Ms. Violet doesn't let anybody tend her yard but herself."

Otho's mind ran rampant. What did the Chief know? What didn't he know? "I did her a few favors." He glanced towards the Sheriff leaning against a wall, arms folded across his chest, eyes narrowed, mean, angry eyes.

"Favors, Otho? What kind of favors?" Mac was smiling but his voice grated at Otho's nerves. "Tell me and I'll help you anyway I can. So will the Sheriff, right, John?"

"Right, Mac."

Otho tried to think but with both the Sheriff and the Chief leaning on him, it wasn't easy. Sweat trickled down his face. He had the money. If telling kept him out of jail, he still had the money.

"Okay." He wiped away the sweat with his sleeve. "Can I have some water first?"

"Sure thing." John opened the door, had a jug of ice water, and paper cups brought in. He and Mac waited as Otho drank a cupful and then another.

"Ms. Violet wanted the body of that guy killing people to disappear." From the corner of his eye he saw the Sheriff move away from the wall.

"Why?" pressed Mac.

"I asked her that as it sounded like a really weird thing to do. She said something about letting sleeping dogs lie."

The Sheriff stepped forward, nodded towards the door. The two lawmen stepped outside, closing the door behind them.

"To get our attention away from the remains in the pond, John. Her sister. Has to be." A shot of excitement quivered through Mac. Finally, after all the years, the mystery was close to being solved. "Why else would she do a thing like that? What else would be so important?"

"She counted on us being so involved in finding Charlie we'd forget about that or it would buy her time to come up with something else."

Mac patted John's back. "Come on, Sheriff. Let's find out what else this young man knows."

"You going to charge him?

"Not yet. If I do we have to read him his rights, get him a lawyer. Let's keep this between friends."

"You can't use any of this in court if you do charge him."

"It's not him I want. It's Violet."

"All right. Let's do it."

Back in the room Mac casually asked, "You spend a lot of time at Ms. Violet's?"

"No, not really." Otho relaxed. "She'd call me, ask me over once in a while."

"What for?"

"Discuss plans."

"You mean about getting the body, where to hide it?"

"Yeah, that's right."
Standing behind Otho, John nodded at Mac, urging him on.

Mac sat down opposite Otho. "How'd you make out with the caps, for the White Squirrel Celebration? Sell a lot?"

"Okay. Why?"

"Just wondering. Lots of folks like you, including us." Mac waved a hand towards John. "We want you do good. We really do."

Otho smiled. "Thanks. I did all right. Made enough to get new tires for the car."

"That's great. Those things are expensive." Mac wished he had a cigarette. Go real good about now. "What else did Ms. Violet pay you for, beside cleaning out the pond?" He managed a small grin.

Otho's eyes shifted between the two men. "What you mean? I already told you."

"Not everything, you didn't, Otho. I'm no psychic but I'd bet my badge there's more inside you just aching to get out."

"Can I have a soda pop, maybe a pizza?"

"Talk first." John didn't want to scare the kid anymore than necessary but his patience was fading fast.

"You heard the man." Mac couldn't get the picture of a smoke out of his mind.

Otho slouched further in the straight-backed chair. "First she tried the fires."

John sprung forward. Mac put a hard hand on Otho's shoulder. "What did she have to do with the fires?"

"Hired me to set them. Didn't want anyone hurt, just get people to quit talking about the pond. Sick and tired of hearing people speculate on who all was down there, she said. Who cared, she said. Must have told me that a hundred times."

Mac released his tight hold on Otho's shoulder. He looked at John. "All right. You'll have your soda pop and pizza. Everything on it?"

"Yeah. Thanks."

Mac opened the door, shouted the order out to an officer, "And make it delivered," then turned to Otho. "Hey, almost forgot - where's the body?"

"In a cemetary."

"Don't jazz me, kid."

"Honest, Chief. Ms. Violet made me wear a blindfold."

Seeing the Chief didn't believe a word of it, he said, "I went in the water, found the body, brought it out, wrapped it in a canvas thing she brought, put it in the trunk of my car. Then she blindfolded me, we got in the car, she drove. When we stopped, she took off the blind-fold and we were in a cemetery. We got the body out of the trunk, carried it over to a one of those concrete things where sometimes people are left instead of being buried, put it inside. She put the blindfold back on me, drove over to her place, I took off the blindfold and went home."

John asked, "What cemetery?"

"How am I supposed to know? I don't hang around cemeteries."

"Come on, John. Let's get out of here."

Outside the room, Mac said, "Have to hold him on suspicion, accessory to arson, body snatching."

"Read him his rights, ask if he wants an attorney. Better call Betty, too."

CHAPTER FORTY-FOUR

Ben caught Lori Anne's pained look when she tried to move her ankle. "Just a minute, honey bun." He took a pillow from Ms. Violet's bedroom, pulled a chair over to Lori Anne and propped the aching ankle on it. "That better?"

Giving a deep sigh of relief, she pulled at the front of his shirt, bringing his face to hers, kissed him on the cheek. "Yes, you big ol' teddy bear. Thank you."

Ignoring the redness growing up his neck as it always did when embarrassed, Ben returned to the wrecked screen door while Bard continued raking glass from the side of the house. Nell took to clearing the dining room still strewn with the remnants of Dawn's mad ride through it.

Lori Anne looked around the kitchen. Maybe when the ankle stopped throbbing she could sit by the sink and at least wash what dishes and such weren't broken.

Meanwhile there was nothing to do but think. Recent events soared through her mind, too much, too fast. Then there was her sister and Frank getting married. Nell and Bard, too. A double wedding! What fun! Wait a minute. If she and Ben were celebrating their life together on a trip around the world why not renew their vows! Three weddings at once. Wow!

Another thought cut into her excitement. Maybe the brides-to-be don't want to share their days.

"Nell"!

"Be right there." Nell scooped a broken vase into a garbage bag, pushed it to the side of the room. Resting against the doorway, she asked, "You okay?"

Lori Anne blurted out, "How do you feel about a triple wedding?"

"A what?"

"You and Bard, Norma and Frank, and Ben and I renew our vows."

"Let me sit down," the word 'wedding' still new to her. "Okay, I'm sitting. Hit me again with that."

"Just what I said. Three couples getting married together before our trip. How about it?"

"Lori Anne, I haven't given the wedding any thought yet. And I'm sure Norma hasn't either."

"What's to think about?" She couldn't hide her excitement. "Unless you were thinking of a big, fancy wedding."

Nell laughed. "I just told you I haven't thought about it at all! But, now that you ask, no, I wouldn't want a big, fancy wedding."

"And I don't think Norma will either."

"I heard that." Norma yelled from the hallway.

As she came in the kitchen, Nell pulled another chair to the table. "Your sister wants to have a triple wedding."

"I only heard that I wouldn't want something."

"Yes," Lori Anne rushed the idea past her. "What do you think?"

Norma looked at Nell. "I don't know. I just said 'yes' to the man a little bit ago. Who's had time to think about the wedding?

"This one," Nell pointed at Lori Anne. "She can't do much else so she came up with this."

"Come on, Sis," Lori Anne stuck out her lower lip. "Please?"

"Stop it, you imp. You know I hate when you pout." She turned to Nell. "She always does that because she knows it ticks me off."

Lori Anne grinned, "Works, too, don't it?"

Now they were all laughing.

"Okay," Nell put up her hands. "Let's ask the men. They are in this, too, you know." Then she asked, "Where's Frank?"

"He'll be down in a minute. Said he needed to call his cousin, PeeWee. He's in Nevada, let him know about - - her." Norma avoided saying what she was thinking.

"Anybody make coffee this morning?" Nell didn't notice the empty coffee pot on the counter.

"Over there," Lori Anne pointed. "You'll have to make more."

Nell spotted the canister and filters nearby. "I'll do it."

While they waited for fresh coffee, the women discussed when, if the men approved, and how all this would happen.

CHAPTER FORTY-FIVE

PeeWee hung up the phone. Frankie's wife wasn't a problem any more. He was free to go home, back to Chicago. An unfamiliar sense of sadness swept over him. He admired, envied what Larry and his wife had, comfortable home, their obvious love for each other. They'd showed him what he'd never seen before, a couple who not only loved each other but actually liked, respected each other.

What could he do for them? Something special. He had friends in Hawaii. Maybe they'd like a week at the best resort on the big island.

Before he could make the call, Maria knocked at his bedroom door. Hiding the loaded gun and holster behind him, he opened the door.

Maria's dark eyes snapped playfully at him. "Come, have wine with us."

Leaving the weapon aside, he followed her down the long hallway remembering when it was Larry he followed.

He'd learned so much since that day. For one thing, now that he knew what a computer was capable of, he wanted one.

Ceiling fans on the patio's cover chased away the day's heat. Larry greeted PeeWee from his wheelchair.

As their friendship grew he'd discarded the usual blanket covering his arthritic legs now dressed in casual slacks. "Let's have a toast, PeeWee." He held up a wine glass.

Maria handed PeeWee a glass, pointed to two bottles on a cart. PeeWee nodded towards the red wine. With his glass full, he held it up. Maria poured herself a glass of the white.

"To our new friend." Larry said in a bold, strong voice. "To PeeWee. May you be in heaven a half hour before the Devil knows you're dead."

The little man laughed. "More likely he's waiting for me."

"Then, my friend, allow me to say, 'May your blessings outnumber the shamrocks that grow and may troubles avoid you wherever you go."

"Thank you."

The three held their glasses together, the crystal singing as they touched.

"I want to do something for you two. You have been so nice, letting a perfect stranger come into your home, helping in every way you could. I want to show my appreciation."

"That's not necessary, PeeWee. We've enjoyed having you. It has been fun having a fellow countryman in the house, cooking for you." Maria offered more wine.

"Yes," Larry added. "Nothing makes her happier than to have her cooking appreciated."

Watching her pour his wine, PeeWee told him, "If I could, I'd take her away from you." He glanced at Larry, smiling back at him. "But I know that is impossible."

Maria stepped to her husband's side, saying softly, "Thank you for the compliment, PeeWee. Someday you will find the one for you."

PeeWee took a deep drink of the wine. Wiping his lips, he grunted, "If I do, she won't be the kind that would have me."

"Ever think of retiring?" asked Larry, holding Maria's hand.

"Ha! That'll be the day. No way, my friend. I've got a city tied up and I plan to keep it that way as long as possible." PeeWee brushed aside where that remark might take the conversation. "I got a friend in Hawaii. Owns a big fancy resort. He'll give you two weeks in the best suite, give you whatever you want. Even pay your airfare, first class."

A silent conversation seemed to be happening as the couple locked eyes. Finally Larry looked at him. "That is very generous of you. We will accept on one condition."

"What might that be"

"You join us there."

Surprised, PeeWee shook his head. "Oh, no. I may not be educated but I know three's a crowd. This is for you, the two of you."

Maria walked slowly towards him, head down, hands clasped demurely behind her. She stopped close to him, raised her head, touched his arm.

"My cousin, Carlotta, she is alone now. She will come, too."

PeeWee looked to Larry who simply laughed. "Might as well give it up right now. Besides Carlotta is an excellent cook and - - ," he quickly assured the nervous PeeWee, "she is much like Maria."

PeeWee's hands went above his head. "Okay, okay. I give up." He took Maria by the shoulders, turned her towards Larry. "Now go back where you belong before I do steal you away. Kidding, Larry. Just kidding."

Picking up the half-full bottle of wine, he headed back in the house. "Decide when you want to go and I'll make the arrangements. Meanwhile I have packing to do."

CHAPTER FORTY-SIX

A phone call from Betty interrupted wedding plans being made. Ms. Violet felt fine, wasn't spending one more night in that hospital, and wanted Betty to pick her up. She'd called her cleaning lady. No need for anyone else to be there.

Betty said Ms. Violet would apologize to Norma and Frank later but right now she'd appreciate it if they stayed with Nell until she had the house back in order.

Norma and Lori Anne exchanged knowing looks, said nothing to the others.

Ben said the screen door was beyond repair, needed a new one. Lori Anne told him to forget about it, Ms. Violet would get someone to do that.

The women put fresh sheets on the beds, carried the used ones to the laundry room and they all left.

+ + + + +

West of town at the Sailor Springs Cemetery old man Kenley, favoring his arthritic left knee, limped towards the only empty mausoleum, the one where Charlie had held Norma captive.

He hadn't been near it since that terrible time, still felt guilty giving that bastard the key, not going with him to the crypt like he should. Didn't want to leave his favorite game show just then. Now the White Funeral Home had ordered it cleaned up for a new customer.

Reluctantly he opened the heavy door, paused staring into the chilly gloom, shut the door, hurried home as fast as that bad knee would allow and called Sheriff Brawley. He hadn't finished his story when John said he'd be right there and hung up.

Soon the phone at Nell's house rang. Hanging up, she told the group, "John has news he wants to tell in person."

The house went quiet as they waited to see road dust announcing the Sheriff's arrival.

Though it seemed forever, less than thirty minutes later everyone was seated in Nell's living room watching John who stood in the center of the room.

Seeing their apprehension he got right to the point. "We found Charlie."

"How?"

"Where?"

He put up a hand. "Hold it, folks. Here it is." With that he told about the caretaker at the cemetery. "So that's the end of that."

Frank broke the shocked silence. "Do you know how he got there?"

"Now that's another story, not one I want to go into right now. Just felt after all you had been through, you deserved to hear this in person." Just then his cell phone rang. He walked into the hallway and came back smiling.

"That's the kind of call I like to get. The school I gave a talk at a couple of weeks ago let out early today. The parents of one of the kids didn't get the word. The kid got home, nobody there. He's scared so did what I always tell the kids, 'When in trouble, call me.' So he did.

" I'll drive over there and wait with him until his mom or dad get home. They both work and I'll find out why they were notified later. Right now I've got a kid to visit See you later."

CHAPTER FORTY-SEVEN

The Early Bird Café was empty except for Betty and one remaining diner.

Anxious to pick up Violet from the hospital, Betty kept busy wiping tables. "Oh, cripe." she muttered as Mac walked in, waving as he took a booth. Violet would be very angry if she didn't get there soon.

Finally the last customer left. She went over to Mac, asked what he'd have but he wasn't interested in eating. He told her to sit down. She listened intently as he carefully explained what had happened.

Betty sagged backwards. She'd tried to help Otho, giving him a nice home though she didn't have much money.

She was proud of him finding jobs, making a place for himself in the community by doing chores for people, especially the elderly, who couldn't do for themselves.

He'd talked about starting a new service, advertising himself as a rent-a-husband for working women.

Now the Chief of Police believed her nephew was involved in stealing a body, setting fires. All her efforts gone for naught.

Mac said she could see him whenever she wanted. Betty said, no, not yet. She'd be by the jail later.

When Mac returned to his office a message from the forensic specialist was waiting. She only had a few more touches to do to the skull found in Soft Pond. Perhaps he wanted to drive down to Carbondale for the unveiling. Otherwise she'd send a photo of the results via E-mail.

At last. He'd know instantly if it was Azalea White. He called John, did he want to go with him. No, John told him, got a court case tomorrow.

+ + + + +

Mac covered the hundred-twenty miles between Olney and Carbondale in record time. He broke that record on the return trip. In the back seat nestled carefully in an unmarked box was the reconstructed skull.

CHAPTER FORTY-EIGHT

First thing Violet did when arriving home after thanking Betty and convincing her to leave, was check her office.

Her eagle eyes scanned the room for signs of an intruder. Next she sat down at the desk, opening drawers, checking their contents. Nothing had been moved. Good. Very good. Now to get the house back in order. A car pulling up in front meant Elsie was there, the cleaning could begin.

Ms. Violet accepted Elsie's concern over her welfare, her dismay at the mess, then told her to start in the kitchen, that she needed to lie down for a few minutes. Elsie offered to bring her a cup of tea but Ms. Violet said no, she'd be okay after a little rest.

Feeling weak, Ms. Violet wanted only to lie quietly in her own bed. The hospital bed had been hard, ought to be a law against such beds, especially in a hospital. And the pillows were nothing to shout about. Awful way to treat sick folks.

She pulled back the bedspread. *The sheets have been changed! How dare those people sleep in her bed. I assumed they'd have the courtesy of sleeping upstairs. That's what guest rooms are for! What else have they done?*

One hand holding onto the furniture, the other on
her chest as though to keep her racing heart from leaping
out, she got back to the office, checked the desk again.
She slumped back in the chair. Thank goodness no one
had invaded her private papers. Had to remember to
keep the desk locked. You got lucky, this time, she told
herself.

CHAPTER FORTY-NINE

Mac entered his office at the police station through the back door, not wanting anyone to see him with the box. Questions that he wasn't ready to answer would be asked.

He needed first to let John know what he'd brought with him.

When he left Carbondale the lab hadn't finished testing a speck of flesh found on a hair still attached to the skull. He needed the results before deciding his next move.

As he sat the box down on the credenza behind his desk his daughter came in from her office.

"Just came from the lab downstate." Cheryl handed him the faxed report.

His eyes went to the bottom line. "Rheum rhaponticum?"

She laughed. "Rhubarb, Dad."

"I'll be damned."

Mac fell into his chair, reading the full report.

"Leaves of the rhubarb plant contain oxalic acid, potassium and calcium oxalates, and anthraquinone glycosides. If not removed before cooking the stalks, causes stomach pains, nausea, vomiting, hemorrhage, weakness, difficulty in breathing, burning of mouth and throat, kidney irritation, and anuria, leading to a drop in the calcium content of the blood and cardiac respiratory arrest. Death caused after long periods of regular ingestion."

Cheryl waited until he put the report down to tell him, "Ms. Violet grows rhubarb. Even force-grows some in her basement in the winter." Having his full attention she continued.

"When I was a kid, I was at her house a lot. Ms. Azalea never refused to play dolls with me and we'd have lovely tea parties under the rose arbor. She loved rhubarb pie, rhubarb jelly, anything made with rhubarb, and, as you know, I had a big collection of Barbie dolls. Ms. Azalea loved them, too, and one day I called her, 'Rhubarbie. She thought that was cute and so it became my name for her.

"Ms. Violet would serve Rhubarb pie, jam, jelly, bread, cobblers, even tea. A real hoot." She saw the concerned look on her father's face. "I never touched the stuff. Ms. Violet said it was a special treat for her sister. She'd make me brownies or sugar cookies. Stuff like that."

Mac's fingers ran through his hair, ending in a clasp behind his head. He stared at her. "See if John would like to drop by."

She saluted and left, closing the door behind her. In a few minutes she reported on the intercom that the Sheriff was on his way.

While Mac waited, he uncovered the box and turned the reconstructed face towards the door, took up the disposable camera he kept for special occasions.

It wasn't long before he heard from the front office, "Hi, Sheriff. He's in his office."

Mac aimed.

The door opened, John took one step in and stopped. Before he said anything Mac had his picture.

"I'm sorry, John." Mac said, enjoying his friend's mouth hanging open, eyes wide. "I couldn't let that look get away. It's priceless."

John glared at him, than with a deep breath, chuckled. "Plain took my breath away." He walked around Mac's desk, taking in the familiar face staring back at him.

Mac handed him the report, denying the urge for another picture.

"Rhubarb?"

"The leaves."

"Ms. Violet?"

"She grows a lot of the stuff, makes jelly, pies, and such from it. Even in the winter. She could have given it to her sister every day for who knows how long."

"Could have been somebody else or maybe the leaves got cooked in something by mistake."

Disappointment dissolved any ounce of good humor left in Mac. "No way we're going to know for sure."

"Afraid not." John pointed a finger towards the box. "However, it will be interesting to see how Ms. Violet reacts when we show her this."

Mac closed the box, picked it up. "Let's go, Sheriff."

"I'm right behind you, Chief."

CHAPTER FIFTY

Out at the farm the three couples were trying to have a normal day.

Nell, with Ben's help, caught up on her chores while Bard and Frank worked in the parlor, each compiling his list of influential, wealthy friends and acquaintances. If the Sailor Springs Historical Foundation was to succeed, researchers, donors, history buffs, philanthropists, were needed.

At the kitchen table Norma and Lori Anne also made lists; who to invite to the weddings, what to serve at the reception, who to cater it, where to hold the nuptials as Sailor Springs had two churches and they didn't want anyone feeling slighted, and most important of all, what to wear.

"This is turning into a job." Norma stood up, stretched arms high. "Remember what Grandma used to say, 'I could stretch a mile if I didn't have to walk back.' Always gave me this silly picture of Grandma, her arms stretched out for a mile."

Lori Anne relished that memory, as she did all of those years. They were so young, so free. The town was their playground, no fears, no worries, only fun. Tears began to form.

She reached in her pocket, fingers feeling for a tissue. She pulled out a piece of paper. "I forgot about this. It was stuck in the back of the bottom drawer in Ms. Violet's desk."

Norma took the paper, screamed, "Sis, this is it!", grabbed Lori Anne, forcing her to hop with her around the room.

Lori Anne seized her shoulders. "Done what?"

Norma let her go. "Mac has always suspected Ms. Violet killed her sister, dumped her in the pond."

"Everybody knows that. He's never made a secret of it. Just couldn't prove it."

"You just did."

"Uh?"

"This," Norma waved the paper in Lori Anne's face. "This is a diary of when and how our dear, sweet Ms. Violet administered poison to her sister."

"What are you talking about? It's a list of recipes for Rhubarb, pies, cakes, cobblers."

"Rhubarb leaves are poisonous. She was feeding them to Azalea every day for who knows how long!" Lori Anne still looked dubious.

"She must have used more of the leaves and that finished off her sister!" Norma yelled, "I know because I used it in a book!"

Stunned, it took a moment before Lori Anne could ask, "Shouldn't we call Mac? Or John?"

"You bet, baby Sis." Norma pointed at the wall phone. "You found it, you tell Mac. He'll let John know."

+ + + + +

As Mac, followed by John, headed for AzLee's B&B his cell phone rang. Lori Anne told of her find.

Mac immediately called John, told him about the call, looked in his rearview mirror and returned his friend's thumbs-up. Both squad cars made a quick change in direction.

CHAPTER FIFTY-ONE

In Nell's parlor, Frank was answering his own cell phone, Aunt Rosie from Chicago. After several minutes of "Yes, Aunt Rosie." "Okay." "I'll take care of it." "Don't worry." "I'll let you know", he hung up, shaking his head. "Me and my big mouth."

Wondering what kind of trouble there was now, Bard asked, "What is it?"

"I shouldn't have told PeeWee about getting married. Now he's told Aunt Rosie. She's having a fit. The wedding has to be in the church, The church, meaning the Catholic Church. With her and all the family in attendance and their best friends of which there must be a hundred or more." He spread his hands out in front of him, fingers splayed, covering the yellow legal pad filled with names. "How am I going to tell Norma? What about you and Nell, Lori and Ben?"

"Well," Bard gathered up the pens and lists. "Guess we'll all have to go to Chicago."

"You're kidding."

"Why not? I've been to several Italian weddings. Just because you're the Godfather doesn't mean you're my only Italian friend. Or don't you think Aunt Rosie will like the idea of three ceremonies at one time?"

"She'll love it. More the merrier for Aunt Rosie. We may have to rent Wrigley Field." He punched his friend's arm. "Come on, Rags. Let's see what the others have to say about this."

They found the kitchen deserted, two coffee cups on the table. Suddenly the thunderous crash of metal on metal shook the cups. Before they reached the door, it sounded again and again.

Frank tore open the door, leaped over the stairs, Bard on his heels.

As they hit the ground the sight of Lori Anne struggling to swing a skillet while leaning on the bat, and Norma slamming a sledge hammer at the iron school bell stopped them cold.

The women saw them, gave the bell one more shot, and waited.

"What the hell are you doing? Scared us half to death." Frank to Norma, Bard grabbed the hammers, tossed them side.

The two women stood shoulder to shoulder smug, identical grins on their faces. Norma answered calmly, "Calling Nell and Ben, wherever they are."

"Good ol' country style." Lori Anne proudly added.

"This better be important, you two." Frank's mind couldn't let go, thinking something horrible had happened.

"It is. You'll see." Norma hugged her sister. "She did it."

"Did what?" Nell asked, coming from the side of house, Ben beside her.

"You'll see." Norma nudged Lori Anne. "Show them, Sis."

Lori Anne handed the paper to Nell, the men peering over her shoulder. "It's a list of things to make with Rhubarb. So?"

"I found it in Ms. Violet's desk."

"You were in her office? She doesn't allow anyone in there."

"I'm the curious type. Sue me."

"I don't get it." Frank took the list. "What is this?"

"Notice the ingredients in those recipes, lots of leaves, Rhubarb leaves."

Nell shook her head. "Nobody cooks with the leaves. They're poisonous."

"Precisely." Norma pointed at the dates running down the side of the paper. "See how often Ms. Violet made these? When one batch of whatever was gone, she made another. She was serving a Rhubarb dish practically every day."

Frank passed the paper to Bard. "Ms. Violet was poisoning - - ."

"Her sister. Had to be."

Suddenly the barking of the dogs and the geese honking warned someone coming.

Rushing to the front yard, the group saw Mac opening the gate, the Sheriff waiting behind him. Neither stopped to close the gate as they drove through, parking close to the house.

Nell tried to hold the dogs but they'd picked up on the humans excitement and wanted to be part of it.

Frank yelled, "Silenzio!" Thunder and Lightening stopped their racket, quieted, tails wagging.

"When the Godfather speaks, even dogs obey." Bard shrugged, Frank glaring at him. "Couldn't help it."

"Never mind," Mac wanted the list, held out his hand "Let's see it."

Lori Anne handed over the list. He and John stepped away to give full attention to the new piece of evidence. No one could hear what they said, only see their heads nodding.

When they turned around, Mac said, "We'll have to keep this, Lori Anne. You did great."

"Tell them the rest. They deserve to know."

"You're right, John. Here it is, folks."

Without telling them about the box in the back seat of his SUV, Mac gave an account of his trip to Carbondale, ending with, "A poison was found in the remains. Rhubarb."

"Hot damn!" Ben slapped Mac's back, then retreated. "Sorry, Chief."

"Don't sweat it, Ben."

Norma had to ask, "Do you have the skull with you?" She motioned towards the SUV.

Mac turned to John who said, "Sure. Why not?"

With everyone breathing down his neck, Mac slid the box from the back seat, holding it while John lifted the lid, slowly brought it up enough to be seen clearly.

One by one they peered at it.

"It is her."

"Azalea."

"Weird."

"Amazing."

"I can't look."

"Beautiful."

Frank's hand slipped around Norma's waist. "Now how did I know you'd say that?"

"Guess you know me too well."

"Do I have to break you two up again?" Mac playfully tugged at them. "Come on, John. We need to get back to town."

"I'm starving," Nell groaned, holding her stomach. "Won't you stay and have something to eat with us?"

"No, thanks. We have some planning to do."

Exchanging glances with Frank, Bard said, "We do, too."

"What does that mean?" Ben said over Lori Anne's face buried in his shirt, avoiding the skull.

John threw a quick glance at Bard, saying,. "Meet you in town, Mac."

Mac closed the box, placing it back on the seat. "See you around, folks. Whatever you're planning now, good luck." He wasted no time getting back on the road.

Lori Anne pulled herself out of Ben's arms. "Can we go back in the house now? It's getting chilly out here."

"Sure, honey bun." Ben kissed the top of her head. "Whatever you got to say, Bard, can it wait until we eat?"

"Of course." Bard said with a wink.

John put a hand on Bard's sleeve. "Got a minute?"

"I'll be there in a minute." He told the others heading for the house. When they were inside he turned to the Sheriff. "What is it? Something wrong?"

"Do you know of any children your father had with women other than your mother?"

"No, but I wouldn't be a bit surprised." He'd learned young to expect anything good from the old bastard.

John fiddled with his hat, brushing the brim, straightening it, brushing it again. Satisfied, he took out the photo, handed it to Bard.

"What's this?" Bard turned it over, read the inscription on the back, took his time digesting what it meant. "My half-sister?"

"Yep. You remember your dad ever going to California?"

"No. He did leave once, took Chuck with him. Didn't say where they'd been when he came back. Mom didn't dare ask." He handed the picture back to John. "Guess insanity runs in the family."

"Don't worry, Bard." John put the picture in his shirt pocket. "It stopped with her."

"Thanks, Sheriff. Now what?"

"Have to catch up with Mac. Got a lot of work to do." He shook hands with Bard. "Take good care of Nell."

"I will. Thanks again."

CHAPTER FIFTY-TWO

No one asked Bard what the Sheriff wanted though Frank gave him a questioning look. Bard mouthed "Later," shaking his head, letting Frank know it wasn't more trouble.

The women fixed a tray of cold cuts and cheeses, olives, pickles, coleslaw, Nell's homemade whole wheat bread, and potato chips. Lori Anne put out a big bowl for the chips, Ben's favorite at any meal.

Before anyone sat down at the kitchen table, Frank said, "This calls for wine."

"Wine? For lunch?" Nell asked, carrying a pitcher of iced tea.

"Everybody sit down and I'll serve." Finding the bottle of Chianti he'd left in the pantry, he opened it, took wine glasses from the buffet in the dining room, placing one in front of each person. With a white dish towel over one arm, he poured the wine with a flourish.

"My goodness, aren't we the fancy ones," giggled Lori Anne.

Norma wanted to know, "What's the occasion?", noting the gleam in Frank's eyes.

When he had filled his glass, he sat down beside her. "We - Bard and I - have news." Seeing concern in the eyes watching him, he quickly added, "Good news."

"If you don't get to it, Francesco Michaele DeCani, I'm going to throw this bowl of coleslaw at you." Norma picked up the bowl, drew back her arm, ready to pitch it.

"Okay, here goes." Pleased she'd remembered his full name, he took the bowl, set it down out of her reach. "First I have to tell you that Aunt Rosie means the world to me. She raised me as though I were her own son. I owe her a lot and anything she's ever wanted, I've done my best to give it to her."

Norma squeezed his hand. "Go on."

"I told PeeWee about us getting married together." He nodded at Bard and Nell. "And about you, Ben and Lori Anne, renewing your vows at the same time. He told Aunt Rosie."

No one spoke.

"To put it bluntly, she wants, rather demands that Norma and I get married in Chicago at a Catholic Church."

Still silence.

"So - ." He looked at Bard for support who raised two fingers in the form of a 'V'. "Bard and I thought we'd all go to Chicago and still get married together, if you don't mind being married by a priest."

Lori Anne took her husband's arm. "Ben, we should renew our vows in the same church where we were married."

"Woman, I'll marry you again any place you want," he felt her grip on him tighten, "so that's what we'll do."

"You're so sweet," Lori Anne cooed, then turned to Norma. "You don't mind, do you?"

Frank clinched his fist as he asked Norma, "What do you think?"

"It would be fun for all of us to be together but" she smiled at the two women, "since it seems I'm getting married in Chicago - - ."

Frank let out a loud sigh of relief.

She gave him a playful poke, "and you want to say your vows here, we'll have to celebrate together later."

"Nell?" Bard leaned against Nell sitting next to him.

She took a moment to answer. "I can't, Bard." Before he could say anything she explained, "I want to be married by my minister in the church I've attended every Sunday all my life."

Bard turned to Frank. "Sorry, friend. You're on your own."

"Wait a minute." Lori Anne put her hand up. "We'll be leaving on our trip soon. Can't we put this off until we get back?

"Of course we can. No reason to rush." Nell grinned at the group. "Unless someone is with child?"

"No!"

"Of course not!"

"Then it's settled. We'll have a big shindig - what, a couple of weeks after you get back, Lori Anne?" Norma knew how jet lag could affect a person, especially after a full month of seeing the world.

"Fine with me."

"Me, too."

"I'm more interested in the honeymoon." Frank leered devilishly at Norma. "Where will it be, my sweet?"

"Stop that! I haven't had time to think about it." She slapped his hand.

"Forgot about a honeymoon. Hot damn!" Ben slapped the table, knocking over the bowl of chips. "We'll have ours in Rome, Paris, wherever we are, Lori Anne!"

She yelped as he jumped up, grabbed her, swinging her around the room.

Bard said to Nell, "May I have this dance?"

"There's no music."

"Listen to my heart." They rose from the table in sync, waltzing into the parlor.

Frank drew Norma closer. "I still owe you a romantic Italian dinner."

America - The Italian Dream
Personal stories of Italians in America.

Because We Are Friends
Leo's articles & short stories including prize winners.

The Saga of Jack Durant
Biography revealing notorious gangster Bugsy Siegel's most trusted friend.

Yahoodywho
Children's story & coloring book of the lion who lost his roar.

Leo's Sailor Springs Series:

Dear Sweetheart
A man's dream of finding his first love results in a torrid affair of seduction, deception, revenge.

Deadly Choices
Left writhing on a bed of silk sheets he turns to murder for revenge.

**TO ORDER THE THIRD BOOK
OF THE SAILOR SPRINGS SERIES:**

DARK SECRETS

Single Book Price:	$14.95
Plus postage:	3.00
	$17.95
AZ Residents Add	
Sales Tax:	.94
Total Price:	$18.89

MIBS Publishing
P.O. Box 17413
Phoenix, AZ 85011-0413

Website: www.booksbyleo.com
E-mail: mibbles@att.net